THE CLAW OF CRAVING

THE FIRST BOOK OF LOST CARCOSA

JOSEPH SALE

Copyright © 2023 by Joseph Sale

First Edition

All rights reserved

ISBN: 978-1-940250-59-5

Cover Art by Kealan Patrick Burke
    https://www.elderlemondesign.net/

Interior Layout by Lori Michelle
    www.TheAuthorsAlley.com

Printed in the United States of America

Visit us on the web at:
www.bloodboundbooks.net
https://www.bloodgutsandstory.com/

"In the black-foaming gutters and back alley of paradise, in the dank windowless gloom of some intergalactic cellar, in the hollow pearly whorls of their slums . . . my awestruck little deer and I have gone frolicking . . . "

—Thomas Ligotti, *The Frolic*

THE STRANGER: "Where blooms the secret flower of the Self?"

—Act I. Scene X, *The King In Yellow*

KIRSTY [in tears]: "Who are you?"

LEAD CENOBITE: "Explorers in the further reaches of human experience. Demons to some. Angels to others."

—Clive Barker, *Hellraiser*

CHAPTER 1:
THE BLACK STAR

THE BROTHEL—although that word did not do justice to the place—was situated in a back alley in a city whose name Alan had already forgotten. He didn't care about where it was, or even its history, only what it could offer him.

The black rain pummelling his windshield mirrored the black storm of his thoughts. He was scared on a number of levels: scared that this place could give him what he sought, but also scared that it would disappoint him. There had been many disappointments on the road to this place, as he followed the whispers of a secret word, a word that tasted like off-milk on the tongue yet still invited him to taste more.

He had sacrificed so much to get to this point. His wife, disgusted by his uncovered proclivities, had left him. His business had failed, more due to his inattention than the embezzled profits. His mother, father, and brother had disowned him. He remembered the very last time he had gone to visit his parents, after his wife had told them what he was; his picture had been removed from the hallway, and their faces had shone with cold light like winter's frost. That was about all he was allowed to see before the door slammed in his face.

Soon, he would run out of money. He doubted he could get employment again. Not because of his secret, for there was no obvious stain on his employment records, but simply because he lacked the strength. He had committed himself to the pursuit of something extraordinary, and it had consumed him.

His hands shook as he waited in the car. He often thought of his hands as independent of himself; his hands were doing the deeds, not him. He smiled at the thought of using that in some kind

THE CLAW OF CRAVING

of legal defence. *Your honour, I tried to stop them, but the hands acted of their own accord, and they outnumbered me two to one.* He had come so far, done so much, it was ludicrous to hesitate now. Yet, he felt afraid.

He'd parked on the main road, perpendicular to the back alley that curved teasingly away from sight. The neon lights of *The Black Star* shone on the dismal brick walls of the tenement buildings that formed the alleyway, a spillage of rainbow, as though the divine beauty of nature could be pierced and made to bleed. It seemed the glow at the end of a tunnel—but perhaps it was rather the headlight of an oncoming train.

"Screw your courage to the sticking place," he muttered. He knew the words were not his own, a quote from some play or book, but he couldn't now think which one.

He forced open the door with a gut-wrenching effort of will. It was ironic that in the early days of his addiction he had tried to exert his will to *resist* temptation. Now, at what had to be the end of his road, either the answer to it all or his total destruction, he had to exert will to *succumb* to his desires.

The rain soaked him through immediately. His long overcoat was no defence against it. Spitting water from his mouth, he ignominiously jogged through the downpour into the alleyway. He could almost laugh. He had imagined his approach to this final destination in a little more grandiose manner, not the scampering of a frightened monkey caught in a storm.

The gutters frothed and gurgled with the rainfall. The brickwork around him shone with mazy patterns in the strange alchemy of moonlight and neon. Rodent eyes blinked at him from under the cover of dumpsters. He imagined the place smelled fetid usually, but the rain was washing that smell away, purging the air. Would that his soul could be purged as easily.

His shoes beat a splashing tattoo on the dirty concrete. The neon light brightened and brightened as he rounded the bend of the alleyway and finally beheld *The Black Star*. Its front was not much to look at. No glass windows with dancing girls, like in the Red Light district of Amsterdam. No gaudy placards with silhouettes of easy women, as in the strip clubs of Birmingham. No plush pink and purple décor, as in the whorehouses of London. A black windowless wall stared back at him. In place of a door, there was a metal shutter, the kind that shopfronts pulled down in rough

2

neighbourhoods to deter theft. The only glamour was a neon sign, spelling out *The Black Star's* name in a font that was almost Hebraic. He saw no bouncer or even a CCTV camera, though the latter might well be hidden. At this point, Alan didn't care if he was caught on film. His life was in ruins. There was only the mystery—that was all he had left. And this place, perhaps it would hold the answer. It had to.

He shuffled towards the shutter and, not quite sure what to do, awkwardly rapped upon it. The clang of knuckles on metal seemed to reverberate through the hissing downpour. He turned, paranoid, expecting perhaps to see the red and blue lights of police cars now following down the alley. But the place was deserted. Even the tenement buildings stood silent. Their windows were occluded, like rows of sightless eyes. He shivered.

He stood in the rain for long moments. He was beginning to grow cold, his bones wetted through as much as his coat. Then, he heard a voice: harsh, guttural.

"Why do you come?"

His heart thudded in his chest. He remembered the first time he had watched porn, waiting until his parents were asleep, creeping to his computer, the adrenaline rush of something totally forbidden. It had been a long time since he had felt this level of childish excitement and terror. It was itself an exquisite sensation, almost worth the journey.

"I seek to go beyond . . . " he answered, surprised by the strength of his own voice. "I seek an experience like no other. To transcend the Self . . . " He wasn't sure about that last bit. He hadn't known he was going to be challenged at the door. He was speaking as honestly as he could, but the truth was that what he wanted couldn't be put into words. He had gone beyond acts that had easy niches and names. There was no category that described his desires. Of this he was strangely proud.

"That is not what you really seek," the voice answered sharply.

Alan bit his lip, looked around, as though expecting to see the answer written in neon somewhere.

"I seek transcendental experience . . . "

A harsh, derisive snort cut him off.

"We cannot help you. If you wish for transcendental experience, go and join a Buddhist temple!"

A monosyllabic bark of laughter, and then footsteps.

THE CLAW OF CRAVING

"No!" Alan said. "No wait!"

He could not see to whom he spoke, but he sensed they had paused before entering some secret doorway on the other side of the shutter. If they left now, Alan knew he would never get to the answer, he would never understand the mystery of desire that had haunted his life like Churchill's Black Dog. Even as a child, innocent, the question had plagued him, caused him to pursue experiences other children would shy away from: eating wasps, smothering his naked body in flower pollen, pouring honey into his eyes. His parents had hoped these were merely symptoms of childish idiocy, and that he would grow out of them. From their point of view, he had, but in reality he had merely become more adept at recognising what was considered socially unacceptable and hiding it from prying eyes. His pursuit of the answer had continued. As a teenager, he had persuaded a girl he was dating to allow him to paint her entire body yellow. He bought her jewellery studded with citrine and yellow quartz. How fondly he remembered Daisy now, his gateway drug.

When his trials with Daisy had failed, her dumping him and calling him a freak, he had investigated other avenues: drinking raw lemon-juice every day for a period of three months, smoking every manner of yellow flower or herb imaginable until he nearly hacked up his lungs, pissing into his own mouth. He had once sunbathed for so long he had given himself serious burns, his body that of a disgusting mummy raised from the dead, the mummy-cloth his translucent, peeling flesh. *I hope I become a beautiful yellow butterfly when this chrysalid is shed,* he remembered thinking. Oh, he had done so much more since then, and still he was no butterfly.

He was crying, he realised. Crying as he stood in a back alley, awaiting something . . . he didn't know what. The rain was cold, but his tears were burning coals upon his cheeks.

"Do you know what you seek?" the voice said, and it seemed to Alan there was a note of softness, of compassion, as though whoever it was had once stood where he stood, had once been lost to the world, lost to self, and lost to God.

Alan swallowed down his emotion. He had to be strong. He had to go through with it.

"What is *Carcosa*?"

With a grinding shriek, the metal shutter began to rise.

4

CHAPTER 2:
THE RITUAL

L IKE A FAMISHED PILGRIM, Alan stepped under the shelter of *The Black Star*, now perceiving who had questioned him. It was a dwarf man wearing all black, save for a bright yellow skullcap. His face was long and sepulchral, with drooping eyebags and a thick, sloping brow, yet he offered a glimmering, goblin-like smile that could not help but alleviate Alan's flagging spirits.

"You have finally arrived," the dwarf said. It seemed his voice was naturally harsh and deep, but now that Alan stood on the other side of the shutter, he heard a lilting music in it as well. "My name is Petruccio." Petruccio extended a hand and Alan shook it. His grip was very firm.

"Are you Italian?"

Petruccio laughed loudly at that.

"Come, the Mistress is waiting."

Alan followed the dwarf to a black door that, even under the neon sign's light, was so well designed that it was almost impossible to distinguish from the wall. With a deft motion of the hand that was unlike the turning of a key or doorknob, the door swung open, revealing a staircase down. The dwarf took the steps carefully—they were not designed for his shorter legs—and Alan followed at a respectful distance and pace. The door swung shut behind them of its own accord.

The walls were brick, but of the faded, yellow kind. Some of them looked partially crushed, as though sagging beneath an immense weight, although that seemed off given that the front of *The Black Star* was only a single storey. There was a crude metal railing on one side of the stairwell, and LED lights flickered on overhead as they descended.

5

THE CLAW OF CRAVING

Alan wanted to speak to Petruccio. He had a thousand questions. But he also felt that if he voiced too many inane queries he would be cast out, unworthy to receive the secrets of this place. Better to remain silent, hold his tongue, and allow the answers to reveal themselves. He had journeyed far metaphorically and literally to get here, paid extraordinary amounts of money to an informant on the dark web for the location. He might as well drink every moment in, rather than grasping desperately for explanations. He felt more able to relax now because that fateful word—Carcosa—had meant something to the watcher at the gate. Alan wasn't crazy, not entirely.

At last, the staircase ended, and Petruccio and Alan came into a hallway of dizzyingly lavish extravagance in comparison with the bare exterior and stairwell. The wallpaper was a deep crimson and the walls hung with paintings that looked like works of the great renaissance masters. Yet . . . when Alan peered closer, their landscapes and figures were far more harrowing and bleak that anything painted by Michaelangelo, Raphael, or Da Vinci. Indeed, the closest parallel that Alan could conjure to mind were the haunting nightmare-scapes of the Polish artist Zdzisław Beksiński. But even they, vivid and beautiful and grotesque as they were, lacked something that these strange paintings evoked with every brushstroke: a sense of ecstatic and terrifying mystery. Yes, it was the juxtaposition of the clarity of the way certain forms were rendered—corpses dangling from a gibbet, locusts filling the sky with glinting wings, monstrous beasts trudging through marshwaters—and the ephemeral and inchoate nature of the backgrounds: clouds where melting cities were glimpsed, where forests faded into wet garden mulch, where solid stone blew away as grey wind—that produced such an effect upon Alan. He stood ensorcelled and mesmerised, unaware that he was rudely ignoring his guide.

Petruccio, however, understood, and waited patiently until Alan was able to tear his eyes away.

"Who painted these?"

"You are not ready to know yet."

His heart thudded even harder in his chest.

"Will I find out?"

"Perhaps. Please, come with me."

There were many doors leading away from this hallway, but

Petruccio directed Alan to one on which a strange sigil was emblazoned. A short line running left to right quickly plummeted ninety degrees downward, then rose at forty-five degrees, then doubled back on itself, crossing the downward line underneath the first horizontal one. If he squinted, it almost looked like an Egyptian Eye of Horus, but reduced to basic components.

"Go through, please," Petruccio said.

Alan touched the door, half expecting to receive an electric shock, and it swung open on easy hinges. Within was a small waiting room, its primary feature a long chaise longue.

"I'll return when she is ready."

The dwarf departed. Alan heard a key turn in a lock.

Letting out a slow exhalation, he sat upon the chaise longue. It occurred to him that this type of sofa was most commonly used in therapy—at least in the stereotypical movies. Hadn't Freud devised this set up so his clients couldn't see his shocked reactions to their confessions? He seemed to remember reading that somewhere.

Alan lay back on the sofa. He knew he was a madman, but sometimes madmen were right, sometimes madmen reached the truth by circuitous means—they gave of themselves more than most people in society were prepared to give. Now there was a thought worth clinging onto.

As the minutes drifted by in waiting, he wondered about petty things. It irritated him that his mind, perhaps on the precipice of a divine revelation, lingered on such sundry details, but he couldn't help it.

He hoped he had enough money, for a start. No payment had been asked for up front when he had booked his "appointment", which was most unusual. He'd had to dial an eleven digit number that he hardly believed was real. To his surprise, a woman had answered. She said very little, merely asking for a date and time. He had given it, she had confirmed, and the call had ended. He had been tempted to redial again to see what would happen, and also partly to convince himself the call had really transpired and wasn't just a figment of his overreaching imagination.

He worried about his body, too. Could he handle it? He had put himself through a lot over the years, and it was beginning to take a toll. He was on the wrong side of thirty-five. *As I approach the journey of my life halfway* . . . That, he knew, was Dante Alighieri. The middle point was where the poet had gone on his epic adventure into Hell. Alan could only pray for such an illuminating experience.

After dismal minutes which seemed to drag on for eternity, the sound of a door unlocking roused Alan from a kind of trance-like stupor of anticipation; the door opened and Petruccio stepped through, a subtle smile on his face.

"Mistress Cali will see you now."

Alan stood on trembling legs.

He followed the dwarf through another door in the crimson hallway and into a corridor similarly lined with exquisite—yet horrifying—paintings. One, in particular, arrested his motion, to the point where he goggled at it like a fish. It depicted the night sky, but looking closer, the stars were alien. A part of him thought this would simply be due to the imaginative faculties of the artist. Why bother laboriously recreating the constellations in their proper arrangement where an astonishing effect might be created with freer placements? And indeed, the effect *was* astonishing. The night was not pure blackness, which might have been dull, but a roiling and layered vista of purple, indigo, and onyx. If he looked closely he could see currents and waves in the darkness formed by the subtle colours, as though it were not the night sky, in truth, but the deep sea. Yet, the stars were not randomly placed. He could see a familiar pattern in them. Was it phallic? These weren't just yellow-white dots of paint scattered randomly on a canvas, there was *meaning* here.

"What you're looking at is *inside* the constellation of Taurus," Petruccio said.

Alan swallowed.

"And that brighter star?"

"Aldebaran. The Eye. Come, my mistress is patient, but hates the unpunctual."

Alan nodded fervently, and set off again after the dwarf.

At the end of the corridor was a black door trimmed with gold. Upon it was the number 0. Given their conversation just a few moments before, Alan could not help but think of an eye, or perhaps a yoni, but that was his desire talking. The excruciations of delayed satiation were now beginning to debase his mental faculties, warping everything into a sexual talisman.

Petruccio opened the door and motioned for Alan to step inside, the sly smile still playing across his otherwise granitic face.

Alan stepped inside and the door promptly shut behind him. Once more he heard the sound of a turned key. He swallowed down a thick bolus of spit, tasting the acid of his fear.

The room was unlike the previous hallways. Sparse, its walls and floor of rugged sandstone. The only illumination came from a pair of twin braziers burning softly at the far side of the room. They were far away, which gave him the impression the room was expansive. The darkness was thick, and even the firelight seemed unable to lift it. His wild imagination conjured the image of an unseen pit just in front of his feet. He nervously laughed at such a primitive fear. This experience might do many things to him, but surely they would not just plummet him to his death . . . Or would they? This operation was undoubtedly illegal, and he a criminal. He had asked for an experience like no other, perhaps death was all that was left to him?

Gritting his teeth with determination, he strode forward into the dark, towards the twin burning lights.

"Stop there," a feminine voice commanded.

He halted, his entire body rigid. The voice had been deep, sensual, authoritative, the kind of voice that emanated not from the throat or even the lungs but the belly, the centre of power.

He looked about him, hoping to see who was speaking, but as far as his eyes could discern, there was no one with him.

"Along the shore the cloud waves break, the twin suns sink beneath the lake, the shadows lengthen—in Carcosa!"

The song caused every hair to rise upon his arms and the nape of his neck. His heart felt like it might explode from beating so fast. Breathing had almost become difficult.

"What *is* Carcosa?" he whispered, unable to stop the question tearing from his lips.

He was answered by a clanging sound. He felt a tightness about his wrist. He looked up in surprise and saw that he had been manacled, a chain descending from the unseen ceiling. A second later, his other wrist was clamped. He let out a pathetic yelp as he was hoisted up, a hidden mechanism raising the bonds; he now dangled by the chains, metal cutting into his flesh.

The darkness before him began to undulate. No, it was the firelight, playing off—a woman's flesh. But flesh blacker than onyx. He had known lovers of every skin tone, but never anything like this. Her skin was darker than tar, darker than obsidian, darker than the abyss. Her lips were the red of menstrual blood. Her eyes were yellow lamps, serpent-like, and painful to look upon.

"I am Cali," she said.

The rational part of Alan's mind reeled, clutching desperately for the sword of truth that would cut through the illusion. A thousand explanations rattled off their hollow litany in his mind: *she is wearing special contact lenses, her skin is painted, you have been drugged*. But the irrational part of his brain told him that this was no ordinary woman, that she had been touched by something beyond the human sphere, something Alan had been searching for his whole life: *Carcosa*.

She was naked, though bejewelled, glorious necklaces and bracelets jangling softly as she moved, their gemstones winking in the flickering light. Her facial features belonged to no ethnicity he could easily place, or perhaps all of them at once. Her body was hard to parse, it fitted so well to the darkness, but he saw voluptuous breasts—and unlike the fakeries of pornstars and prostitutes, these swung low, nearly to the belly button. Her hips were so wide it was as though they were made to girdle the earth. Her forehead, where the third eye was said to reside, was marked by a yellow spot. Her proud lips pouted like flowers, and her eyes revealed to him the sacred mystery of his own thundering heart.

Breathless, he waited for her to speak, or sing, again.

"Alan Chambers?" she said, after what seemed an age.

"Yes." A whisper.

"You have been seeking me, or rather, seeking what I guard, for a long time."

"*Yes.*" He could have wept again. He could not believe it. He was *here*. He stood at the final threshold, the final gateway to the Infinite he had always craved.

"What you are about to undergo is known as the Ritual of Five. Should you pass the ritual, you will be bestowed the Yellow Sign, and granted entry into Carcosa."

Alan's mind spun. Carcosa was a place, *a place*. It seemed so obvious, but the fragments he had collected over the years had woven words such as Carcosa, Hastur, and Yhtill into sentences and allegories too complex to fully unravel their meaning. All he had known was that in them lay the answer to the riddle of his own strangeness.

"But you should know that few pass to the fifth level," she

continued. Her eyes bored into his. She had not yet blinked. "Some perish in the attempt. Most simply fail. Of course, losing their goal, having come so far, drives many to take their own lives." She paused, allowing the gravity of those words to sink in. "This is your very last chance to turn back, Alan. If you choose to go forward, there is no telling what you will become."

"I am ready."

"Are you sure? Remember, this is your last chance."

Alan smiled, a Satanic rictus.

"Do with me what thou wilt!"

CHAPTER 3:
THE FIRST THREE LEVELS

CALI SMILED. His words were performative, so he understood something of ritual. Heavy-lidded, languorous, she regarded him for a few moments more, then turned and walked away into the darkness. The sight of her retreating, though it afforded him a brief, pleasurable view of her shapely buttocks, soon became an agony. He had gazed upon a soul-searing beauty, and to lose it was torture.

Soon, however, she returned. She carried a jewelled knife.

She approached him. Her scent was excruciating. On the one hand, she was fragrant, like a rose. But beneath that sugary sweetness was something like meat, as though she had recently chewed raw flesh. While at first it repulsed him, soon it drew him in. He found himself inhaling more deeply to drink its richness again. The effect was like visiting the countryside, the way that farmers and countryfolk seemed to *enjoy* the smell of manure—it spoke to them of a living Earth, of fertility and fecundity, whereas to Alan's citybred senses all he discerned was shit. With Cali's strangely rotten aroma, he found the same conversion occurring within himself; its unpleasant notes suggested something deeper, something he longed for.

She kissed him on the neck—a vampire's kiss, perhaps—and he felt a jolt of electricity run through his whole body. His arousal was painful.

"Let's free you," she purred.

With delicate motions of her knife, she cut away his clothes. She lastly removed his shoes and socks. This gesture, so simple, yet seemed so deeply intimate. The discarded garments fell to the floor like a snake's shed skin. *Finally, the chrysalid is sloughed off,* he thought, and a smile came to his lips.

12

Cali perceived the smile and returned it with her own. Her teeth were impossibly white, glimmering and carnivorous.

She stroked his chest with her free hand. Her touch was so soft it sent shivers through him.

He was not overly muscled, but he kept fairly fit. At one point, his obsessive pursuit of the truth had led him into yoga—for it was, after all, intimately connected with the occult—and he practiced every day. This had given him a degree of physique, which Cali now admired, stroking his stomach, then moving lower to his throbbingly erect penis.

"The first level is the level of Earth," she said. Just before her fingers would make contact with his member, she took them away—a tease. She walked slowly around him. He could do nothing, suspended as he was. He could feel the blood leaving his hands as circulation was cut off. He cared nothing—he had endured far worse discomforts. In fact, his old fear was beginning to return that this might not be the answer, that ultimately this was all a theatrical ruse. If he'd wanted to be tied up and play some kind of BDSM game, there were a thousand prostitutes who would serve the need. What he wanted was Carcosa, what he wanted was *magic.*

Cali now stood behind him. He felt her breath—strangely scented as her body was—on the back of his neck. Her hand circled his torso, stroking his chest again. He felt her breasts pressing into the skin of his back, so deliciously full. Her lips caressed the top of his spine, then between the shoulder blades, then lower still, upon the coccyx . . . Alan felt as though he was vibrating, both with the tension of being suspended and the expectation.

"Now," she said. "Let us begin."

The hand that had stroked down his chest now gripped his cock and he gasped for the pleasure of it. Meanwhile, her lips moved down to his anus. She began to stroke while simultaneously he felt her tongue licking his secret orifice. He had given and received analingus in the past—even considered himself an expert in it—but what he experienced now shocked him. Her tongue penetrated him with a small stab of pain—this he was used to—but then plunged deeper . . . and deeper . . . He whimpered now, her tongue thicker and longer than anything he had previously been penetrated with. All the while her hand continued to rhythmically stroke his member, which had become simultaneously as hard as a rock and silky smooth, as though her fingers were turning the clay of his being into wetted putty. She was kneading him into a new mould. The tongue continued to explore him, deeper and more fully than he had ever been explored. He felt her hot breath, the wetness of her extraordinary tongue. Surely, there was some trick here, no human tongue could be so long. Yet he felt it curling and coiling in him, licking.

Yes, there was pain, but the pleasure overrode the pain, the way the moon could eclipse even the brightest sun.

What sent him over the edge was her moaning sounds—deep, animal—as though she, too, were experiencing the same kind of physical ectasis from giving him such pleasure. He shot his load into the darkness and cried out, his voice reverberating strangely off the stone walls.

His body gave one great convulsion, then he hung limply in his chains. Slowly, the tongue was withdrawn. He fought to keep his eyes open, light-headedness and exhaustion overtaking him.

Cali appeared in front of him again, her lips glistening with spittle. She wiped them slowly with the back of her hand.

"The first level is easy. The second will be harder."

"I'm ready," he said.

She smiled.

"Yes, I believe you are."

His manacles opened, seemingly of their own accord, and he dropped to the ground, nearly losing his balance with surprise. His arms tingled with pins and needles, his fingers arthritic, flexing awkwardly. He tried to shake them out, but the blood would only return at its own pace.

"Come this way," she said.

She turned and walked into the gloom. This time he did not have to watch her go, but hurried after her. His mind raced as he walked across the stone floor, his feet stung slightly by the cold. What he had experienced was deeply pleasurable, but could it really be considered magical? Again, he feared the hollowness of reality.

Abruptly, Cali stopped, and it took Alan a few moments to see why. Before them, a part of the floor *did* give way to a pit, just as he had childishly fantasised. No, not a pit, but a *pool* of ink-black waters, long and thin like a bath.

"These are waters from Lake Hali," she said. "Enter and ablute yourself."

Alan nodded. He strode forward and began to lower his foot into the pool—sharply, he withdrew. The water was colder than anything he had known; it made his skin feel like it was constricting, cleaving against his bone so powerfully that it stabbed from within.

"So cold," he said.

Cali looked at him without expression.

He tried again, forcing his foot and ankle into the waters. He let out a gasp, then gritted his teeth and pushed down until the water reached his knee. The pool was not deep; his sole found solid ground. But his leg was numb to the top of his shin. He tried wiggling his toes and could barely tell whether they moved.

With grunting effort, he managed to slide his other leg into the pool.

"In," she said, without mercy.

He nodded, teeth chattering, knees knocking together. The cold was spreading even where the water did not touch, creeping up his legs, shrivelling his manhood, which moments before had stood prouder than it had in a good few years. He squatted, putting his arse into the waters first, then finally lying back, stopping just before the waters went over his head. He shrieked, at this. It felt like a noose around his neck. His fingers reflexively sought the edges of the pool and gripped them. Cali paced toward him, crouching low.

"Head. Under."

He took three quick breaths to steady himself. The cold was indescribable, invasive—more invasive than Cali's freakish tongue. It felt as though his cells were dying every second he languished in its death-grip.

With a final breath, he plunged. The cold swept over his entire body. He fought down the scream that desperately wanted to tear from his sealed lips. He was fully immersed. His sense of direction, even his sense of self, was immediately destroyed. He could not feel his limbs. He could be thrashing yet would not know. He could have broken his fingers on the hard stone walls of the pool and not realised. All striving was pointless. He had to give up fighting. He had to give up *everything*.

Entombed, cocooned, he allowed the absolute void to envelope him. He had, of course, experimented with sensory deprivation, but this was a deeper experience. Whereas the sensory deprivation tanks merely robbed one of aural awareness, this seemed to create a void within his physical body. As the pores of his skin drank in the water, little emptinesses appeared inside of the dim throb that was all that was left of his awareness; he could feel them, in that they did not feel of anything except pregnant potential. In that sense, he was expanding, filled up with darkness, the gaps between his cells widening and widening as gulfs appeared . . . He was coming apart, and there was a strange beauty in that.

The numbness gave way. Someone was with him in the darkness. Hands, hands gripped him, and he was rising. His sense of place and direction were restored.

His mouth opened involuntarily and he heaved in a lungful of air. He had not felt the need of air, down in the dark, but now it was as though he'd been submerged forever.

His eyes opened and the firelight, dim though it was, shocked him. He had to close them again.

Cali hovered over him. Her skin glistened with liquid. She had hauled him out of the pool. Did that mean he had failed?

Her smile said otherwise.

"How long do you think you were in there?"

He blinked. The loveliness of her face was incentive to regain the use of his eyes.

"I don't know. A minute?"

Her smile remained inscrutable. She straightened, extending a hand down.

"Come. The third level awaits."

Staggering on limbs rendered clumsy with cold, he followed her to another invisible pocket of the mysterious room in which there lay a stone slab like an altar. Manacles extended from the four corners of the altar. It was clear he was meant to lie upon it.

She waited for him to clamber awkwardly onto the altar, then swiftly set about strapping him down. She pulled the chains tight, spreading his limbs similar to the Vitruvian man.

Cali produced her jewelled knife once more. "The mind is the sword that cuts to truth."

He was not alarmed to hear her utter something so close to his own thoughts only a few moments ago. It was an old esoteric truism. However, the blade in her hand chilled him. How literal would her interpretation be?

16

She inverted her grip on the dagger, angling it downward. The point hovered over his solar plexus.

He wanted to say: *Wait,* to beg with her, but a deeper self held him back. Did he really want to stop her? What if this death would be his release into a new life? He had interviewed countless Near-Death Experiencers on his quest to find whispers of Carcosa. Only one, an old woman called Beatrice who had been resuscitated after an astonishing five minutes on the other side, had given him any kind of clue.

"Strange is the night where black stars rise," she'd intoned, her eyes clouded, staring off into some unknowable space. When he had pressed her for more information, she'd simply said, "All answers lie in Carcosa."

Could it be that in her temporary death she had glimpsed the land of Carcosa?

Could it be Alan needed to die to go there?

He steeled himself, his every muscle rigid with tension, trying with all his will to master the death-terror.

"Truth," Cali whispered, and plunged the knife into his stomach.

Alan screamed in agony. Only the hilt protruded from his flesh. A dark smile lit her face with black radiance.

Slowly, as though it gave her erotic pleasure, Cali began to draw the knife from the wound. Blood foamed. Alan thrashed in his chains. And then, the knife slid from him with a squelching noise.

He gasped.

There was no wound. Skin had sealed perfectly where the knife had once been.

His heart pounded. His limbs trembled. This, this had to be magic. Still, the sword of his intellect started to cut to and fro, looking to part the veils of illusory reality and find desperate solutions behind. *She has drugged you. These are special effects and the pain is psychosomatic. None of this is real. It's all a hallucination.* But none of these explanations could dispel the sensory reality of what he was experiencing.

"Again," he whispered, faintly.

Cali smiled, and drove the knife down a second time, this time into his thigh. He shrieked like a banshee and she pushed deeper still. Alan frothed at the mouth with inexpressible pain as blade touched bone. The violation of that penetration was an affront to biology. The cold kiss of metal on marrow would remain with him for the rest of his life.

She withdrew, the wound healed, and he stopped thrashing, dragging air into his lungs with heaving breaths.

Now Cali climbed up onto the altar with him, crouching between his legs. His cock stirred, despite the fact he had so recently spilled his seed, and endured such pain. Her heavy breasts stroked against his legs as slowly she moved upward toward him. She planted a kiss on his belly button, then lower, then lower again. She made soft purring sounds as she did so that stirred him again into a frenzy. She took his cock in her hands and held it near the base, though it would have remained furiously upright had she let it go, such was his arousal. She opened her lips and allowed a long, spidery drizzle of spittle to baptise the tip of his penis. Then she pushed her breasts together, enfolding him in sheer voluptuousness. She stroked her soft breasts up and down, and he closed his eyes to enjoy the peculiar but ecstatic sensation.

Pain of a different caliber brought Alan back to reality.

He screamed like he had never screamed. His voice rose three octaves, producing a thin, reedy, squealing sound. His eyes flashed open and he saw that his penis, stroked to a hardness and length rarely achieved even with drugs, was pierced horizontally by Cali's blade, the tip of the knife poking out one side. She smiled cruelly at him.

"*No*, no . . . " he whimpered. He couldn't writhe or shake this time, any slight movement would wrench the knife and tear him apart. He was paralysed in a paroxysm of pure and unending agony. Blood poured from the wound alarmingly fast.

"Now, intellect must conquer desire," she said.

She climbed off the altar and left him there, gasping, nearly blacking out with the pain, his life-force running out of him.

"No, Cali, please . . . "

She returned moments later with a basket full of needles. These were not like acupuncture needles, with which Alan was familiar, they were two centimetres thick and six inches long.

"I can stop this," Cali said. "But you will have failed the Ritual, and will go from this place never knowing the truth of Carcosa."

Alan stared into her lambent eyes.

"No . . . " he choked. "I go on."

She stroked his brow, the way a mother might an ailing child. "Good."

One by one, she inserted the needles into his body. The first was just above the genitals. The second, underneath the belly button. The third into his solar plexus—breathless, a gargling sound escaped his throat.

The fourth, she punched through his sternum. If he had thought the blade nicking his femur was excruciating, this was another level. Bone gave way beneath her uncompromising strength.

"Chin up," she said.

At first, he thought she was trying to give him hope, then he realised she meant it literally. Dreading what was to come, he lifted his chin. The needle pushed through the calcification of his Adam's apple into the soft flesh of his throat. He spluttered and blood flew from his mouth. He was, by this point, drenched in his own scarlet life-source, suffering the unnatural sensation of being clammy within yet hot on the surface—he was warming himself outside-in.

"This next one will be . . . strange," she said.

He could barely nod or speak. In fact, he could barely think. His body was a column of agony, a totem of cruelty. He felt as though there were electrical currents passing through and between the spikes, shocking him, making his spinal column an energetic highway.

She covered his mouth with one hand, and even though his vocal chords were partly destroyed, he managed a wheezing scream against her fingers.

She pushed the sixth spike into his forehead. He hoped his skull might offer some resistance to her, but no, bone gave way like cracking an eggshell. His pineal gland was skewered. Now, involuntarily, he began to jerk, an epileptic seizure. Visions flashed, not before his waking eyes, but across his inner one. A black lake, twin suns reflected in its onyx mirror-surface. A city—a city of nightmarish architecture that yet impressed upon him an otherworldly beauty, the way that a crow, tearing the entrails from roadkill, still wears the colours of a gorgeous midnight. White foam dribbled from his mouth. He choked nonsense words.

"One more, my sweet," she whispered.

The final nail went through the crown of his head, down into the brain. At this point, blackness took him. He drifted upon invisible currents in the void. Winds struck him from all sides, winds made up of the voices of the damned. They spoke a language he did not know yet felt he recognised, and that with time he could understand, for it was buried in his own DNA. He was soaring and falling at the same time—he cared not which—and if there was a bottom to this pit, he felt no fear. Something rushed up from beneath him, a Shadow alive and vast as the universe itself. The greatness of this dark being took his breath away. It swept him up in its invisible grip and now he was certain he *was* flying, flying upward, in the arms of darkness . . .

He woke. All pain had left him. He lay upon the altar plinth still. His body was whole and had been washed, for a wet and reddened sponge lay to one side along with a pile of seven needles.

Cali stood over him. For a second, he thought she held a look of concern, a slight furrow of her prominent eyebrows, but then the serene mastery returned, and she was the living goddess unperturbed by his mere mortal struggles.

"You have passed the third level," she said.

CHAPTER 4:
THE FOURTH AND FIFTH LEVEL

H E WAS WEAK with blood loss and the psychological horror of his ordeal, yet he had committed, and there would be no respite until it was done.

"Are you ready for the fourth level?"

"I am."

Cali stepped back from the plinth.

"Then prepare to be burned in the Fires of Ecstasy."

He lay for a few moments, wondering if something had gone wrong. But then he began to notice that the plinth on which he rested was warm, unnaturally so. He looked at Cali; she stood by, impassively watching him. Did he detect a note of trepidation, perhaps an unwillingness to leave him to his fate? No, this was mere fantasy—he was falling for the otherworldly woman, despite the fact she was author of his pain (or perhaps because) and projecting his own desire onto her impenetrable facade.

The warmth steadily began to mount, until his flesh was stung by the heat. He found himself involuntarily writhing and fidgeting, the way a sunbather on the beach might when the sand scorches them. *Fight it, Alan. Lie still.* He knew, in part, this was not just about passing the trial, but a desire to impress Cali. He forced himself to lie still, locking his limbs rigidly. The heat grew, until it far exceeded discomfort and became active pain. He *couldn't* be still, not when it felt like his flesh was being melted.

It was only going to get worse.

He shrieked as flames erupted, bright tongues licking his entire body. He did not have presence of mind enough to wonder how solid stone was burning. His intellect had finally abandoned him. He gave no thought to hidden compartments or gas pipes leading

21

into the plinth. The stone was on fire and he was lying atop the stone, bound to it—that was all he knew. His skin did not blacken or even redden at the touch of the fire. He felt the agonising pain, but there was no damage. Yet, that did not reduce his terror, for the pain continued to climb as the fire burned more fiercely, and where normally he might have perished from the burns, he could not die, and therefore his pain could only increase. Nor did it seem possible that he would black out. He had to endure this with waking alacrity. Flames scoured his eyeballs. Tongues of fire flayed his back. They licked his genitals like the barbs of a nine-tail whip. His every pore drank in the torturous fire.

"I . . . I can't . . . "

He thrashed to and fro. He screamed. Every time he felt he could contend with the agony, it increased, as though in proportion to his inner endurance, as though measuring him with calculated malice.

"You must learn the lesson of the flame, or you *will* be lost," Cali said, her voice stern as steel.

The lesson of the flame? How could he learn anything? Every time his mind tried to revolve upon an issue, pain interrupted it, overwhelmed him.

Overwhelm . . . Was that, perhaps, the point? He had to stop fighting, stop believing he could master the pain, to *surrender* to it.

Alan closed his eyes and purged all thoughts. Instead, he directed his attention to the sensations. He focused in on each individual agony, one by one. He embraced the excruciating sensation of the flesh of his back peeling, the feeling of his genitals being boiled. His eyes were two burning rocks scorching the inside of his skull, soon to melt into slag. The more he focused on the sensations, however, the more he found they paradoxically started to disappear. It wasn't that he was numb, it was more that the closer he inspected the sensations the more illusory they became. It reminded him of a book he'd read on quantum physics: the closer scientists looked at atoms, from electrons to quarks, the further they drilled down into the components of matter, the more it seemed matter did not really exist.

He squealed, but this time with delight, as he realised that without really willing it he had transformed his experience. What he had mistaken for pain was actually *pleasure*. The flames were, as Cali had promised, ecstatic. His entire body convulsed in the preliminary throes of an orgasm. He let out a victorious cry as he came, his seed swallowed by fire.

Slowly, the flames died down, the ecstasy bled from him, and he was once more lying on a bare plinth, though it retained some of its warmth. Cali approached, smiling down at him.

"Few pass the fourth trial. You instinctively leaned into the pain. That is most unusual."

"Part of the reason I have come here is to understand my own strangeness," Alan said.

Cali smiled.

"It is the only strangeness worth knowing."

"What is the fifth level?"

"You will see."

Cali loosed his bonds and advised him to wait. When she returned, she was bearing a black robe.

"Put this on."

He did so, finding it to be extremely comfortable, the material unlike anything he had ever worn before, perhaps closest to silk in texture.

Cali led him through the darkness towards the two burning braziers he had spied upon first entering the room. *Twin fires for the twin suns,* he realised. It was a neat bit of symbolism. But what did the twin suns mean? He had seen them, briefly, as she had jabbed the needle into the top of his skull (he found himself gingerly touching where the needle had pierced, thinking he might find a scar, but there was none). Past the braziers was a staircase descending into a yet lower level of the structure. *The Black Star* descended perhaps three or more storeys deep.

The stairs were shorter than those to reach the initial crimson hallway, and revealed a beautiful room lit by four flames, one burning at each corner. Apertures in the ceiling swallowed the smoke. There was a slightly raised dais on one side, and a mat upon the floor woven with patterns in black and gold that defeated any attempt to decipher them. On the dais, there was a collection of strange instruments.

"The fifth level is spirit, or ether. This level is unlike the others, in that it is not so much a trial of endurance, but a test of something less . . . material."

"I understand," Alan said, although he swiftly realised that he did not understand at all. Cali seemed amused by his faux pas.

THE CLAW OF CRAVING

"We will see. Please, sit upon the mat."

Alan sat down cross-legged. The robes, and his yoga training, made the motion fairly natural and easy for him. Cali climbed onto the dais and picked up an instrument that looked a little like an Indian sitar. The wood from which the instrument had been fashioned was unlike any he had seen, hornet-yellow and porous like flesh; whomever had crafted the instrument had not seen fit to polish or smooth the wood, so that gnarled excrescences projected from the body. In one place, it seemed fungus was blooming, neon-bright frills decorating its already bizarre exterior. Stranger still, the instrument's neck was curved like a scimitar, and the strings *curved with the neck*. Alan frowned. Surely, such a design could not produce any meaningful sound? He counted twenty-two strings in total, one more than a traditional sitar.

Cali sat cross-legged, facing him. She rested the body of the instrument against her left foot, holding it diagonally across her torso. A thrill of excitement, quite different from his erotic arousal, passed through him.

"I will perform the Song of Yhtill for you." Her eyes bored into his, holding him with the mesmerism of a snake-charmer. Yes, he was the phallic snake, and she, its master. He had met many enthralling women in his life, women whose sole devotion had been the art of seducing and bewitching souls, but he had never been so intoxicated by beauty or intrigued by mystery as he was now.

The first note she plucked nearly knocked him unconscious. It was a sound he had no words for. He had a basic grasp of music, but it was no note he recognised, it had no place on the harmonic scale. And from that initial sound came a multiplicity of resonances, as though from the eternal oneness there emerged children of reflected light. The splinter of the note into a self-harmonising chorus seemed to splinter something within Alan. He gasped for the sheer power of it, shaking crown to root.

But Cali was only just beginning.

With fingers impossibly dextrous, she began to play notes of mind-bending ethereality. No sooner did they come into being than his brain reeled in incomprehension. Her music could not be called a melody, not in Western terms. It most resembled the haunting sitar-work of Ravi Shankar, and the Indian gurus of music, some of whom were said to possess magical powers as a result of their understanding of the ancient ragas. But Cali's music transcended even that. The impossibly curved instrument, carved from the wood of a tree that had no name, produced a sound not of this earth, and not of human understanding. The sound was synaesthetic: the notes had colour, shape, taste, and feeling. Each chord conjured images from the grave of the unconscious, resurrecting memories from their sepulchres, and washing him with sensations not of the body but of the soul. Black seas roiled within him. He burned in the heart of a dying star. Purple winds scoured the landscape of his mind. Faces metastasised and then disintegrated into nothing. His flesh was peeled back to reveal the grinning skeleton beneath. All these visions and more afflicted him with each trembling note of the haunting music. But they were more than visions; they were lived.

The sound was a labyrinth, and he its explorer. The notes seemed to—quite literally—hover in the air, like spectres of those he had left behind on his journey to reach this sublime moment. At times the chords she played stabbed him like needles, they were so clear and sharp. Other times, she used her elegant fingers to bend her notes, and with it, the walls of their inner sanctum seemed to bend, the tongues of flame to bow as if stirred by a wind, the shadows created by those fires to move of their own sinister accord.

The sound rose like a storm.

Acutely, a terrible sense of *indefiniteness* assaulted Alan. It was the feeling that if he were to put his hand on the floor, his hand would pass right through it. The walls seemed translucent, and beyond them, dark stars wheeled and gurned.

The instrument exerted a dreadful power. He felt paralysed, hypnotised. But more than that, as he watched Cali in all her black and enigmatic splendour striking the strings, he felt a strange identification with her instrument. Blinking, he seemed to see *himself* in her arms. His belly had been opened by a knife. His ligaments were stretched over the strange, curving neck of the instrument, and these she plucked to produce such alien sounds. The neck? It was his own spinal column. The body of the instrument had been fashioned from his ribs. And his wide-open mouth emitted the ghastly droning of a universe beyond the known. His entrails writhed in death-pulse contortions to the stertorous rhythm, which had no beginning and no end, for it was the sound of existence itself, stranger than the blackest heart, emerging out of the womb of the void.

He had been screaming for five minutes and not known it.

There was drumming now, and dimly he perceived that Petruccio was by his mistress's side, beating an ancient tabla with what looked like human bones, its battered-head made from flesh pulled taut.

Cali's voice broke through the madness.

"Song of my soul, my voice is dead, Die thou unsung, as tears unshed, Shall dry and die in Lost Carcosa!"

Every hair on Alan's arms stood and he cried out. The ceiling blew away, and above them the gulf of eternity throbbed with dismal life. Stars winked like cyclopean eyes.

Cali's litany continued. *"He has bathed in the waters of Hali, and burned in the Fires of Ecstasy. He has lowered himself to the coprophage and raised himself to the martyr . . . Great King In Yellow, grant him entrance into your kingdom!"*

A terror seized Alan. He had come too far. He now teetered upon the precipice of human understanding, to go any further was to go beyond the limits of his species. He had to turn back, he had to flee, to forget he had ever heard the word Carcosa, forget he had ever been fascinated by the colour yellow, forget himself with liquor or drugs or women and never again probe that which should not be known.

"Cali!" he cried.

Her eyes met his. The music's storm had become a hurricane about them, stripping away the feeble veil of reality, revealing something deeper beneath, something livid and pulsing like maggots in a wound. Her yellow eyes held him, upbraided him for his cowardice.

Hold, Alan, they seemed to say. *Hold.*

"I . . . I can't . . . " The fear had consumed him.

"You can!" she said, out loud. "Hold!"

The visions he now saw, crowding around their little room, were impossible. Hideous towers broke a sky choked with yellow clouds. Double suns glared down from the heavens like wrathful eyes. And the sounds . . . He did not know whether it was Cali and Petruccio's music that created the illusion, but he thought he could hear a city, the screaming, yawing, jabbering-mad cacophony of an asylum-citadel.

Alan stood, the effort like lifting a planet, unsteady on his feet as the maelstrom shrieked its reality-tearing fury around him, dragging colour and form into the abyssal sky. The bleak shapes of a new reality remained behind a wall of movement. The centre of a cyclone.

"No!" Cali cried.

Everything lurched, a tremor passing through the floor—if such a thing existed—and Alan stretched out his right hand to steady himself. His hand passed through what should have been a solid wall, what *had been* a solid wall before Cali started playing her infernal song.

Alan screamed, withdrawing his hand—except, there was nothing to be withdrawn. His wrist ended in a blackened stump. Pain shot through his nerve-endings all the way up his arm, to the shoulder, and into the brain. Fried, screaming, he fell to the ground kicking like a beetle overturned on its back.

"He has paid the price!" Cali called, into the storm. "He has been marked. Great King, now grant us entry!"

And before Alan's stunned eyes, the world he knew disappeared with all the ceremony of an email deleted, and in its place, a festering splendour arose: so awful, so majestic, and so terribly beautiful that he could not help but offer libation to its glory in the form of burning tears.

CHAPTER 5:
THE YELLOW SIGN

ALAN LAY THERE for a long time, clutching his severed stump. The pain died down surprisingly swiftly, leaving only a dull ache. Whatever magic he had unwittingly interfered with had cauterised his wound. However, there was an ugly yellow mark upon the blackened flesh; at first, he thought it was an infected scar, pustule-coloured and weeping. But he soon realised it was no scar but a *brand,* a brand in supernatural colours. The Yellow Sign. Carcosa had marked him now. He could never return to whom he had once been.

And was it not fitting that his *hand* of all things had been taken? The tool with which he had so desperately grasped at the truth, at reality, had been destroyed.

He lay on the flagstones of a ruin upon a hill. Crumbling walls surrounded him, formed from yellow brick. Strange weeds grew from between gaps in the stones, their flowers curiously fleshy.

Cali stood before him, though now she was clothed in purple robes that shimmered, semi-translucent, about her body. She looked regal, a queen. Her magical instrument was slung over one shoulder, the way a travelling minstrel might wear their guitar. Petruccio was clad in the same black garb and yellow skullcap he had worn when he first greeted Alan. He had strapped his drum upon his back.

"Welcome to Carcosa, Alan," Cali said.

Alan rose shakily, clutching his wrist.

Cali's eyes flicked to the missing limb.

"You have given much to come here. But do not worry, you will find many things here to replace what was lost."

Alan nodded, not sure what to say, what to believe. He had

wanted this his whole life, yet now he couldn't help but query his sanity. The overriding question in his mind was not "Where am I?" but "What have they done to me?" Was he lying somewhere in the basement of *The Black Star* hooked up to a drip-feed of psychedelics?

No. Though the doubt would take some time to dispel, his deeper intuition told him this was real. He could feel the stone beneath his feet, and the wind . . . it did not taste like anything he knew.

Cali walked up to him and placed a hand upon his shoulder.

"Behind you there is a door. Why don't you go through?"

Alan turned. The ruins did indeed have a doorway. Yellow light shone beyond it. He looked at the sky hovering over the ruins and saw a blackness broken by pinpricks that were vaguely familiar . . . The painting! He remembered it had shown the view of Taurus from a planet within its dire constellations. Was that Aldebaran he could see, shining like a cursed diamond?

Now his fear was beginning to melt away, alchemically transformed into excitement. He was *here*. He had arrived. This was his journey's end. The answer to all the riddles!

He strolled boldly through the door and almost fell down, overwhelmed by what he saw.

The ruin upon the hill overlooked a sprawling city that made the densely populated enormity of Tokyo seem but a rural town. Its walls rose a hundred feet high at least, resembling vaguely the wall of Jerusalem, but greater in height and width, and eschewing the organised beauty of its stonework in favour of something altogether more disturbing to the human eye. The city's spires were numberless, making the skyscrapers of New York seem quaint. Unlike those huge modern towers, these erections curled, abutted the sky with spikes, leaned at angles that should have been architecturally impossible. Some were bulbous like mosques, others jagged as the most Gothic of churches. All were fashioned from the same yellow stone as the entire city. A xanthous jewel shining at the heart of a desert.

From every spire, crenulation, and window tattered banners blew, a thousand, thousand shades of yellow, many of which had no equivalence or name in the world Alan had left behind. Carcosa blinded him with hideous arrogance.

"What . . . what are those . . . ?"

"The bodies piled against the walls?" Cali had come to stand beside him.

Alan swallowed and nodded. There were thousands of corpses—stacked nearly to the full height of the wall. Their yellowed flesh was sloughing, liquefied, meaning that the corpse-pile seemed more like one entity with many eyes and mouths than numerous dead. Indefinable shapes crawled over the rotten mass.

"There was a battle, not long ago. You will learn more about it, but first things first, we must take you to see Cassilda."

Alan turned sharply.

"I have heard that name before. It was . . . it was her song you were singing."

Cali smiled.

"You will hear many things you have heard before. Carcosa leaves its traces wherever those who have been marked by its beauty tread."

Alan looked down at the Yellow Sign, carved into the burned flesh of his maimed limb. He was a gimp, an amputee. Carcosa had left its mark. Was it worth it? Did it matter if these were his final days?

Cali began to laugh, light and coquettish.

"What's funny?"

"You think that you're at the end, don't you?"

"Yes," Alan said weakly.

Cali's smile widened.

"Come, you will see the city, and then we will meet the Princess."

She led Alan and Petruccio to a stairway that zig-zagged down the hillside. As they descended, their perspective changed, and Carcosa's immensity seemed even greater and more daunting.

When they reached the desert floor, Alan realised they were not the only ones approaching the gargantuan city: pilgrims marched clad in grey rags, dragging carts behind them full of what seemed to be ornamental wares, though they were unmistakeably *organic*: they stirred sleepily like children on a long journey; richly bejewelled merchants in gossamer robes rode upon black-furred camels with five legs, their satchels jingling with gold and promise; and bands of men and women in turquoise kaftans bent their heads against the whispering winds, speaking to one another in a language Alan did not recognise. If the other travellers found Cali,

Alan, or Petruccio strange, they gave no sign, but continued on their way in loose columns, eyes fixed upon the city's spires.

"Where are they coming from?" Alan whispered to Cali.

"From Yhtill, from Demhe, from Hali, from secret, underwater Alar," she answered. "And even from the lands of Pe'kar, though those last are unlikely to gain admission in a time of war. All souls wend to Lost Carcosa, the greatest and worst city, the brightest and dimmest . . . "

As they neared the wall, Alan saw a massive gateway, larger than the Arc de Triomphe. It towered over the wall. Dark shapes stalked across its upper battlements, their spears glinting like rose-thorns in the light of a morning sun, banners trailing from the hafts, flapping in the constant wind. Underneath the gateway were more guards. Their armour made them seem inhuman creatures (though perhaps they were), plated and bony, more like carapace than metal. Indeed, as they drew closer, Alan saw the armour *was* fashioned from the exoskeleton of some colossal insect, chitin slabs linked into overlapping plates and scale-mail. Spikes protruded from odd angles. The helmet, presumably the head of the insect itself, rose in a high triangular crest. Every piece was unique.

There were about ten guards at the gate. They stopped all who approached. The many columns of travellers and pilgrims all united into one stream here, sucked into the sinkhole of Carcosa's mouth.

He was now close enough to hear the city's clamour rising from beyond the walls. He'd heard an overture of it in the Song of Yhtill. Now, to waking ears, the noise was a sensory assault. The closest approximation was the inside of a hornet's nest, a vociferous buzzing, but this accompanied by the blaring of discordant trumpets, the tolling of rancid bells, and the shrieks of the dying.

They watched as the group of travellers in turquoise approached the gate. They were too far to hear what words were exchanged, but it seemed they were denied entry. All of a sudden, things became heated. Several guards came forward from where they had been lurking in the shadow of the gate. The turquoise travellers refused to budge. Perhaps they had travelled so far they would not be turned away? Seconds later, there was violence. One of the guards brought his spear down in a slash and opened the neck of one of the travellers. The others shrieked and fled, but spears—hurled like javelins with unerring accuracy—followed them, impaling. Blood drenched the sand. The few survivors ran for, of all things, the corpse-piles, perhaps intending to scale the walls. Footing was treacherous. One slipped and slid down the mulched flesh and gore, landing back at the feet of two guards, who promptly finished him with downward thrusts of their spears. Another almost made it to the top, scrabbling like a cat up a crumbling cliff-face.

It was then Alan spied one of the dim figures he had seen from a distance, crawling over the corpse-piles. He mistook it at first for an insect, a dung beetle perhaps. But in fact all its features were human, they were simply arranged in the wrong quantities and order. Its face and torso were supported on six arms, each ending in a grotesquely oversized hand. There was an anal orifice at its rear, but no legs. Its face was smeared with gore and lacked all human intelligence.

It raised its eyes to the intruder climbing its hill and let out a blood-curdling shriek. Moving with alarming speed for something so haphazardly made, it bounded forward and leapt upon the kaftan-wearing traveller, pinning him in the dead-slush. His gargling screams continued for many minutes as the creature sank its teeth into the nape of his neck, tearing with its plenitude of hands, until there was nothing but a flayed corpse.

Alan turned and vomited onto the sand.

Petruccio laughed.

"I threw up myself the first time I saw one."

Alan wiped the sick from his lips with his sleeve.

"What are they?"

"Volunteers?"

"I'm sorry?"

"After the battle, they beseeched the King In Yellow—*Deathless be Him!*—to change their forms. They wanted to be of service after the battle . . . "

Alan's mind reeled.

"But who would choose . . . "

"Hush now, we approach the guard," Cali said, ending their exchange.

"Halt!"

One of the insect-clad warriors strode towards Alan's party, clicking as he moved. His spear was still wetted with blood. Human features were just discernible beneath the sloped visor.

Cali stepped forward. The watchman regarded her.

"Princess Cali, you have returned . . . "

Princess? Alan wondered. *Was she royalty?*

"My business is urgent."

The watchman bowed and stood aside. She strode through the gateway. Alan's guts twisted. Was she leaving him here? Would he be turned away or killed? What would be worse, to die by the spear or be doomed to wander the desert forever under strange skies, not knowing how to get back to his own world . . .

The watchman turned to them. His flesh, like Cali's, was onyx-black. But if he held any respect for his "Princess", it did not extend to her companions.

"Only those of royal blood or marked with the Yellow Sign may enter the city."

Petruccio stepped forward. He removed his yellow skullcap, revealing a patch of shaved scalp. Inscribed in glowing scar-tissue was a sign like the one on Alan's wrist, though different in ways almost too subtle to express. The Sign was made up of five lines, and with a jolt of memory, Alan realised where he had seen it before: inscribed on the door of the waiting room, where he had mistaken it for the Eye of Horus.

"You may pass," the guard said. The dwarf bowed and set off.

Lastly the guard turned to Alan. Alan held up his stump.

White teeth showed. A grin.

"You've been marked deeper than most. I can tell this is your first entry to the city. Know that the life you once had is deader than the wastes of Demhe. The Yellow Sign makes you a stranger in your homeland, wherever that may be. You belong to Carcosa now, and to the Yellow King—*Hideous and Bright Is He!*"

The guard stepped aside.

Alan bowed, aping Petruccio, and then strode forward. As he walked through the mighty arch, graven with images he could not comprehend, the sound of the city rose and rose, like the furious cheers of a coliseum throng welcoming their champion home.

CHAPTER 6:
WHAT IS PE'KAR?

THE CITY, THE CITY, the city. There was no truth but the city. There was no reality but the city. It was both body and tomb, asylum and palace, inner sanctum and outer space. Every brick was alive. Indeed, some of the stones of the city's walls and buildings had faces that moved, spitting curses at passersby. The streets were arteries carrying payloads of jabbering merchants, civilians, and creatures to and fro. The buildings were cancerous tumours rising to lofty heights, overgrown with flora at once mycelial and anthropoid. From every window of these towers, voices called and banners flew.

Any other city cursed with such twisting and organic architecture might have found its streets predominantly in shadow, but the twin suns, shining ghastly and pale in a sky that otherwise seemed taken over by Night, washed the city from every angle in a kind of bleached effervescence. The city itself was luminous too. Spires pulsed like lighthouse beacons, sending gibbous flashes across the metropolis. Church bells sounded and momentarily the streets changed colour, becoming rivers of quartz flowing to an unknown source. The bright jewels of the city's denizens winked like captured stars.

Cali and Petruccio waited for Alan to recover from his shock. At last, he mastered himself.

"It is . . . "

Words failed him.

"Awful and wondrous and hideous and beautiful," Cali supplied.

"Yes, all those things, and more."

"You shall have a small tour of the city, on the way to the

palace. Of course, you shall not see even a hundredth of Carcosa's splendour, but it shall serve at least as an introduction."

Alan nodded, and the three set off. He noticed that many stood aside when Cali strode down a street, signalling she was indeed descended from some kind of royal lineage. Alan longed to ask her about it, but he was so overwhelmed by all that he was seeing he did not have the presence of mind to form questions.

"There are five Orders of Being in Carcosa," Cali said. "See, over there, those feasting on excrement? These are the coprophages."

Alan's nose winkled. The reek of the shit-heaps these naked men and women were hungrily lapping at would have disgusted a fly.

"Then there are the outcasts." She indicated a huddle of individuals in various types of garment. Some wore the pauper's dress of medieval peasants. Others bright kaftans and robes. Some wore items that looked almost like the modern day clothing of Earth. "These make up the majority of Carcosa's population. All pilgrims and travellers here are designated as outcasts; that includes you and Petruccio."

Alan laughed bitterly.

"What is funny?"

"I've been an outcast all my life. And even here, in another universe, it is the same."

Cali smiled.

"Ah, but here, outcasts make up the majority, like I said. You are not perhaps as alone as you might think."

They continued through the city.

"The third order, the courtiers, are subtly distinguished from others. These have royal blood in them and are obligated to serve at the palace for at least a portion of their long lives. For some the term is a thousand years, for others ten thousand . . . "

"I'm sorry, did you say *ten thousand years*?"

Alan knew a little about the mythological chronology of ancient Egypt, with rulers such as Agathodaimon reigning for a hundred and forty thousand years or more, but he had believed that to be mere exaggeration or metaphor. He was unable to comprehend that span of time in relationship to the life of one individual.

"Ah, yes, you must adjust your sense of time. Don't worry, it will happen naturally—*in time*." Seemingly pleased with her little paradox, Cali let out a bright laugh that was then answered by the thunder of bells. They had passed by a church. Its exterior was carven with images of tentacled beings, nude women, and figures in mysterious robes.

"The fourth order of being are the shades," Cali went on. How she was navigating the streets was a mystery to Alan, for he was already utterly lost. In any city one might expect to find crossroads, and in England there were roundabouts with many turnings, but here it seemed every few paces there was a bifurcation of routes into an infinite multiplicity. He passed under miniature arches only to glance back over his shoulder and see new streets—streets he had certainly never trodden—where he had just walked. Once, he glanced between two buildings and saw a secret alleyway leading to a colourful bazaar, but when he blinked and looked again there was a staircase, and looking a third time he saw a door.

"You will not see the shades, for they walk the city invisibly."

"So how do you know they are there?"

Cali smiled.

"How do you know you love someone?"

"By . . . feeling?" Alan blushed. Cali's ravishing beauty had eaten into his soul; he was infected by it.

"Yes," she said. "Close your eyes, Alan. What do you feel?"

He felt rather stupid, doing this in the middle of the street, but he stood still and closed his eyes. For a few moments, there was nothing. He felt the wind, tugging at his robe. He felt the dull throb of his maimed limb. His breaths, flowing in and out slightly quicker than normal. His heart continuing its song.

"I don't . . . " But he stopped himself. He *did* feel something, as though people were brushing past him in a busy city centre, London or Paris. An ephemeral yet intimate crossing of destinies. He opened his eyes and found he stood alone; Cali and Petruccio had moved off to one side, leaning against the wall of a building that itself was leaning at a near forty-five degree angle.

"Did you feel something?" Cali's eyes bored into his, and he wondered if there was not a hidden question beneath the one she asked.

"Yes," Alan said, hoping it was not his imagination.

"Good. So, you have become acquainted with the fourth order." She motioned for him to follow and he scampered along. They broke from their quiet street into an altogether more chaotic one.

Petruccio suddenly scarpered off, hailing a bearded merchant in lilac robes, and then conversing with him furiously.

"What is he doing?" Alan asked.

"He has business in the city," Cali said. "You did not think this was purely a holiday trip, did you?"

Alan smiled, for the first time in long years.

"No," he admitted. "But it is strange, even for someone like me, to believe this is real. We are so conditioned to accept limits on what is possible. They ram a material worldview down our throat from the very day we're born. They destroy the palaces of imagination until there's nothing left."

Cali showed teeth, her expression one of aquiline pride. She turned and motioned with one sweep of her elegant hand at the sheer expanse of the city.

"Forgotten, perhaps, but not destroyed. Does this, to you, look like a ruin? Does it look, to you, like the palaces of imagination have crumbled? Behold them in everlasting splendour! Behold them in undying hideousness! *And praise be to the Throne of Carcosa, that shall never yield!*" As she spoke, a dark light—like the twilight of an eclipse—shone from her flesh. A wind rose and suddenly her hair and dress were a shimmering cloud about her radiant form. Alan could not help but fall to his knees, such was his terror and awe. Likewise, the strange inhabitants of Carcosa bowed, humbled and obeisant as the goddess blazed like the fell star of Aldebaran. The flashing terror of her eyes struck Alan like a lightning bolt. He saw her rage and sadness and hope, written there in starlight, scouring his falsities.

And then the moment passed, with the ephemerality of a dream. She stood before him, Cali again. Resplendent, beautiful, but still. The cityfolk roused themselves and continued about their curious business. Alan sheepishly got to his feet.

"I . . . I'm sorry . . . "

"No," she said. "You spoke in ignorance, not in malice. And it is true that your world has suffered of late. Fewer and fewer come to *The Black Star* seeking this path. But perhaps, Alan, that is why you are here. Perhaps you, like Jonah, will bring word to Nineveh of the coming of the Lord . . . "

Her smile was like a secret flower.

Petruccio returned, shaking his head, and—to Alan's irritation—taking Cali's attention from him.

"You did not find what you sought?" Cali inquired.

"He did not have it. But he had heard a rumour from Yhtill . . . "

"Well, then what you seek is almost certainly *in* Yhtill," Cali said, laughing gayly. "Rumours always turn out to be true. Alan will attest to that!"

All three smiled. Cali led them on. They rounded a corner and came into an area of the city where the crowds thinned almost to nothing, and the architecture subtly changed. Whereas most of the city was wrought of yellow stone, these buildings were black and oily, as though they bled. There was a reek about the place, even more astoundingly awful than the usually pungent scent of Carcosa.

"The fifth and final order are the cannibals," she said, as though it was a matter of little concern.

"Jesus!" Alan cried.

A naked man, crawling on all fours, had crossed the street in front of them. His hair was tattered and long, his body lean yet muscular, corded tendons standing out under the pale skin. Tattered flesh hung from his pearly teeth and blackened gums. His eyes were cocaine-white and senseless.

"They represent the void," Cali said. "Without which order has no meaning."

Alan was keen to hurry on out of the district of cannibals, but Cali walked unafraid.

They came into what seemed a market square, though they had passed many courtyards, forums, and gardens that could have served the function just as well. A crowd had gathered.

A wooden gibbet rose in the middle of the square like the sea-rotten bones of a whale. A man in bright yellow robes was reading from a sheet of parchment to a crowd of onlookers. Another man stood with his neck in a noose. He showed no sign of fear, but stared blankly ahead, like one spaced out on ketamine. A third, wearing all-black with a pointed executioner's hood, stood to one side beside a fateful lever.

"His crimes are as follows . . . " The man in yellow proclaimed. "Worship of the most foul and hideous demon, Pe'kar!"

At this, the crowd hissed and booed. Strange fruits flew through the air and struck the soon-to-be-hung man in the face. He did not flinch, but continued to stare resolutely ahead.

"Inciting others to worship thy false god!" the accuser continued, his voice rising an octave with each criminal act he described, as though his outrage were rousing him to near hysteria. "Treason against the Most High, The King In Yellow—*Deathless be He!*—and conspiring to overthrow the Throne of Holy Carcosa."

Alan leaned over to Cali, not taking his eyes over the bizarre medieval scene.

"What is Pe'kar?"

Cali's jaw tightened.

"It is best not to ask such questions in public, lest you attract the attention of the executioner." It seemed as though the terrible shadow in the pointed hood turned hungry eyes upon Alan in that moment. He shuddered. "I shall answer you, so that you need not make a fool of yourself in future," Cali went on. "Pe'kar is a demon who claims to be a god. His lands—named after himself in sublime arrogance—lie far, far east of here, across the desert of Demhe. He is the sworn enemy of Carcosa, and he will stop at nothing until he either has the city in his power, or is trampling upon its ruins."

It chilled Alan to consider that a city as mighty as Carcosa could face such an enemy.

"Why does he hate Carcosa so?"

Cali's lips curled in a dark smile.

"It is not the city he hates, so much as the ruler."

"The . . . The King In Yellow?"

"*Hideous and Bright Is He!*" Petruccio murmured. Then he looked sharply at Alan. "Best to add praise whenever you say His name, son!"

Alan nodded.

"Therefore, by the Laws of Most Holy Carcosa, and the authority of the Yellow King—*Everlasting His Name!*—I sentence thee to Death!" The man in yellow robes finished with a dramatic flourish, and made a chopping motion with one hand. Unceremoniously, the executioner pulled the lever. The criminal—without a word or cry—dropped through a trapdoor. There was no *snap*; the rope had been too short to break his neck. His legs kicked involuntarily as he asphyxiated, but his eyes remained austere and unfazed, as though he had claimed an inner kingdom for himself that could not be breached by the woes of the world.

"We had best move on," Cali said, delicately. "For now the executioner will be about his bloody work."

Alan saw the hooded man sharpening two cruel and serrated knives. Yes, he did not want to see the drawing and quartering—he hurried after Cali.

CHAPTER 7:
THE PLAY

THEY ENCOUNTERED ANOTHER market square, but instead of a gibbet, this one featured a wooden stage. A group of mummers stood upon the boards, wearing gorgeously elaborate costumes that would not have been out of place at a Venetian masquerade. There were two women, and one man, and the scene they were acting out appeared to be that of a ball. One woman was clad in a golden, corseted gown with a train so long it would have been suitable for a wedding. The other wore a black dress that seemed more like the bandages of the dead. All three actors wore pale masks, the kind used in ancient commedia de'arte or Japanese theatre, bearing exaggerated and fixed expressions. The open mouths of the masks presumably amplified the speakers' voices.

Alan was pleased to see that the play was better attended than the execution.

"May we stay and watch for a little?" Alan asked. "I feel I may learn more about Carcosa . . . "

Cali sighed.

"You will glean little truth from this farce," she said, and her tone was uncharacteristically bitter. "But I suppose it will do no harm."

They situated themselves near the back of the crowd. Cali and Alan were both tall enough to see over the heads of those in front. Petruccio grumbled. Alan wanted to offer him to sit upon his shoulders, but thought better of it.

The two women were deep in conversation on one side of the stage. The man stood to one side, his mask fixed in a leer so grotesque it was demonic.

"Camilla," the woman in gold said. Her mask portrayed an expression of innocent delight. She moved with exaggerated elegance, gently embracing the woman in black. "Dearest mother, who first bore me into the world. Say, what troubles thee? Thou hast been most melancholy at this joyous occasion! Can it be that thou disapprove of my choice of husband? Can it be that thou hast doubts and misgivings?"

"Fairest daughter, Cassilda," Camilla answered, her voice deep yet ethereal, the mask producing a strange echoing effect. It was contorted in a frown of perpetual sorrow. Alan noted that Cali's fists were clenched. He wondered what it was about this performance that so irked her. "Most dear to the heart of our great Lord. Thy intuition has led thee aright. I am plunged into the deepest pits of sadness, for when thou art married, thou shall be gone from me. How can'st I part with thee, whom I suckled at the breast?"

At this the man stepped forward to the front of the stage and turned his leering mask toward the audience, a comedic aside in Shakespearean style.

"Would that I could'st suckle at those breasts!"

A smattering of crude laughter rewarded this jibe.

"O Mother, thou art the kindest and loveliness soul in the world! Put off this face of sorrow, for it is but a mask thou wear'st!"

To Alan's surprise, Camilla, the woman in black, did indeed remove her sorrowful mask, revealing a face of haunting, autumnal loveliness, pale as moonlight, the reflection of her youth's glow, but strangely *more* beautiful because of it.

"Likewise, dear daughter," Camilla said, stroking Cassilda's mask. "Thou must put aside thy innocence, and for thou merely masketh thy true feelings. Is there no sorrow in thy heart to leave mother and father behind?"

Cali mouthed along with every word, yet her fists had become white-knuckled in their tightness. Alan dared not speak. The crowd was pin-drop silent.

Cassilda nodded slowly. Then, she removed her mask, revealing her face, a spring-time beauty of youth yet marred by glistening tears. What a fine actress she was, the picture of innocence teetering on the brink of loss.

"Even my lascivious heart is quelled by those tears!" the man said, again making an aside to the audience. "How can I covet a figure so fair and delicate with these grasping and monstrous hands?" He held them up in front of him, the grotesquery of his mask now seemingly directed at his own limbs. "Shall I make amends?"

"Of course I do, mother," Cassilda said, sobbing now. "I will miss thee until the Black Star itself dies, robbing the sky of supernal light!"

Cassilda and her mother embraced. The mother, too, shed tears. There was a smattering of polite applause from the audience.

Camilla turned sharply, then, towards the leering man. He stepped forward sheepishly, his body language perfectly conveying the guilt of one caught eavesdropping.

"You, sir, should unmask."

A tense silence greeted these words. Alan's spine tingled. The audience seemed to know something was coming. Perhaps they had seen the play before, or perhaps it was simply the premonition inherent to all sapient beings of imminent catastrophe. His heart pounded and his mouth was dry.

"Indeed?" the man said. His voice! How it had changed, now laden with threat. A pall of dread descended over the audience, a stillness so absolute it seemed eternity waited upon the actions of mere mortals.

"Indeed," Camilla persisted. "It is time. We have all laid aside disguise but you."

The man made no motion.

The mother stepped forward. She reached up and touched his face, and then a shriek tore from her throat and she fell down upon the stage. Cassilda screamed, throwing herself down upon her mother, as though to protect her. Alan recoiled, horrified. The mask upon the man's face—it had moved! And now Alan realised the dreadful conceit of the scene. What had seemed a mask, impossibly grotesque, impossibly pale, impossibly contorted, impossibly frozen, was in fact a *real face*.

"I wear no mask," the man whispered.

The audience had become a frenzy. Children screamed. Men and women threw themselves down upon the market cobblestones and bashed it with their fists and foreheads. Others fainted.

"No mask?" Camilla cried, gripping Cassilda as though she were the edge of a cliff. "No mask!"

"Ah yes," Cali said. "Act one, scene two. I must say, of all the play's lies, this is my favourite,"

"How . . . " Alan whispered. "How did his face do that?"

"They train for centuries," Petruccio said. He alone seemed unmoved by the play. He had found a stone bench to stand upon to afford him a better view. The revelatory horror had disturbed him very little; in fact, he seemed bored. "The mummers. They are more magicians than actors as you would think of it."

"I see . . . "

The play went on, each scene that followed more elaborate and strange than the last. Some segments were performed in languages Alan could not understand. Others were rendered entirely nude. Alan discovered that the male actor was freakishly well-endowed.

Despite Cali's initial unwillingness to stop, they stayed until the interval. The two women who'd played Camilla and Cassilda disappeared into a yellow tent behind the stage, but the male actor descended the ramp and greeted his audience. He made his way through the crowd and intercepted Cali, Alan, and Petruccio.

"It's rare I have a royal audience," the actor said, dripping with charm, offering a formal bow. Now that he was off-stage, he looked entirely different. Everything from his manner of speaking to his walk had changed. Alan was simply amazed by the elasticity of his expression, both his body and face pliable to any shape. Resting, his features were quixotically handsome: a chiselled chin, a sharp nose, a rogue's smile, and electric eyes. "I am The Stranger, as you already know . . . "

Cali rolled her eyes, though she seemed flattered by his attention. Jealousy surged within Alan like a serpent. Then he chided himself. Cali had made no promises to him, in truth; he had no claim on her. And besides, jealousy was a poison to the soul.

"You played the role of The Stranger so well," Alan said. He hoped the compliment did not sound like it was coming from between clenched teeth. "I'm sure my question is primitive but . . . how did you speak whilst not moving your mouth?

The Stranger smiled at him. God, his handsomeness was a wound to all other men!

"I thank you, but it was no role: I *am* The Stranger."

"A thousand, thousand men and women claim they are The Stranger," Petruccio said. "And I've yet to meet the 'real' one."

"Then you have misunderstood The Stranger's creed," the actor said, unfazed. "We are all The Stranger in His many guises. I *know* that I am merely an actor, who was named LeBarron by his mother in a moment of hilarious irony, for our family was very far from the riches of a baron indeed, but *through me* The Stranger completes His glorious work."

"It sounds more like religion than art," Alan said.

The Stranger—or LeBarron—smiled.

"Isn't the greatest art *always* religion?"

"I hate the play," Cali said. "But you did play it well. Here . . . " She produced a coin from her glittering robes. "A token of royal favour." She flicked the coin toward LeBarron and he caught it.

"A most gracious gift." He bowed. "From the hands of the greatest beauty in Carcosa."

She extended her hand and he kissed it.

"I am a writer as well as an actor," he said. "And I am working a sequel to *The King In Yellow,* did you know? I seek to rectify some of its injustices . . . I call it: *The Queen in Black.*"

Cali laughed.

"Men have been hanged for less."

LeBarron grinned.

"Yes, well. They shall have to catch me first. And it is difficult to hang a man when you don't know what he looks like." Before Alan's stupefied gaze, LeBarron's face transformed. His eyes seemed to move closer together, his nose wrinkled up until it was a snout, and his lips peeled back, revealing the fish-face of a simpleton; Alan *knew* the character immediately even though he didn't have a name to go with it: the kind of shut-in who lived their life through movies and video-games and feared reality with a passion, allergic to real experience. But the genius of LeBarron's performance was that Alan felt no dislike for the character. On the contrary, he saw a piece of himself in this man, and recalled a childhood avoiding his parents, avoiding his teachers, avoiding intimacy with friends, all for fear they would discover the rotten soul he was beneath . . . He had been this man, once upon a time. And perhaps there was more of the man left within him than he cared to admit.

A moment, and the illusion passed, and LeBarron was himself again, although Alan began to wonder how one could ever know *who* LeBarron really was, given how plastic his being seemed; he was more water than man, filling up a cup, taking on whatever shape it presented to him.

"Well, I shall leave you now," LeBarron said. "But I hope our paths will cross again in future." The actor's eyes, surprisingly, lingered upon Alan. "You have a strange aura about you, Alan Chambers. I would like to play you one time, with your permission, of course."

With that, he departed into the crowd.

Alan stood there, stunned.

"He . . . he knew my name."

Petruccio and Cali exchanged a glance.

"Perhaps there is a trace of The Stranger in him, after all?" the dwarf said.

Cali snorted.

"We shall see."

The trio journeyed on, through the labyrinth of Carcosa's streets, until finally they came upon the palace. In any other city, it would have been visible for miles, but the army of towering spires and churches of Carcosa, so clustered together as to defy architectural sanity, denied them view until the palace came upon them suddenly. Alan's mouth opened. Just when he thought nothing could now shock him, the city outdid itself, striving to please him like an ardent lover.

The palace resembled a ziggurat, though it bore features alien to that art of construction. A staircase—consisting of many thousands of steps—led up to a columnated entryway. A temple-like building crowned the pyramid, a jewel set upon its brow that sent disfigured yellow light in blasting rays across the cityscape. The proportions of the entire structure were beyond comprehension. Its mountainous enormity seemed to steal the light of the twin suns.

Gardens flowered across its upper levels. Many of the flora and fauna contained in these looked carnivorous, their petals ornamented with teethy extrusions, their stigmata dripping sweet scents and venomous liquids. Every inch of stonework was engraved with hieroglyphics, searching eyes, and scenes sourced from every conceivable mythology. Massive lizards sunned themselves on the steps; they loosely resembled Komodo dragons except that spiny sails extended from their backs, flashing the entire hue of the rainbow-like ostentatious fans coveted by nobles. Masked courtiers passed by these giants without fear.

"Behold the palace of my Father," Cali whispered. Even she seemed awed by its sight, or perhaps she was lost in a memory.

THE CLAW OF CRAVING

Everything clicked into place.

"You hate the play because they left you out of it," Alan said. "You're Cassilda's sister!"

Cali smiled.

"He's sharper than the last one," Petruccio said.

Alan's heart did a somersault. *Last one?*

"Hush now, Petruccio. He has only just pieced together one puzzle. No need to present him with further riddles."

The dwarf bowed, though he fixed Alan with a meaningful stare for a few moments. Alan could not read what his expression meant. Not all could bend their face like LeBarron, and make it speak louder than words.

"Come, my sister is waiting," Cali said.

They ascended the steps. Alan decided to query Cali a little further.

"May I ask why they slighted you?"

Cali smirked.

"I am the black sheep of the family, both in form and function."

She would say no more than that.

After a gruelling climb, they reached the palace itself, though on their way they passed many doorways that suggested the ziggurat had many levels within it, a vast and complex network, each part of the palace accessed by a different type of functionary. Both Petruccio and Alan required a few moments of rest at the top of the palace, exhausted from the long ascent. By this time, the twin suns were setting over Carcosa, each one finding a different home on the horizon. Their diminution was more than compensated for by the appearance of a grisly moon. It resembled the moon of Earth, except that a great dog had taken bites out of it. No clean sickle, but a half-eaten holy wafer.

By its side, the Black Star of Aldebaran shone freakishly bright.

For the briefest moment, Alan thought of what had once been his home. Where was Earth in this black expanse?

Then he laughed, knowing he would never willingly return.

CHAPTER 8:
CASSILDA

AFTER THEY HAD RESTED, they ventured within. Pillars thicker than some skyscrapers, impossibly grand, held up a stone sky daubed with murals sickeningly colourful and bright, oppressive in their splendour, as though the artists sought to humble those who gazed upon them with the zealotry of their brushstrokes. Alan noticed Petruccio studying the images, hardly lowering his eyes to see where he was going. At one point he produced a small leather-bound journal, inkwell, and a quill. Managing to keep pace with Cali's long strides while juggling the objects, which indicated to Alan a degree of practice, Petruccio dipped the nib into the inkwell and began to make preliminary sketches.

"You're an artist?" Alan said.

Petruccio grunted, absorbed in his work.

They passed thousands of courtiers and perhaps fifty guards on their way into the inner sanctums of the palace. Finally, they were greeted by a mighty set of doors, wrought of some metal for which Alan had no name or archetype. The engravings upon the door were dazzlingly vivid, depicting tens of thousands of figures, all engaged in microcosmic stories, and above them all, a broodingly vast god, robed in tatters yet crowned by a five-pointed star.

"Is that . . . ?"

"Don't speak His name, not so deep within the palace," Petruccio advised.

Alan could not take his eyes from the engravings, not simply because of their infinite complexity—the more he zoomed in, the more there seemed to be hidden in the metalwork—but also because of what he sensed on the other side. LeBarron had used the word "aura" when speaking of Alan. Alan was no tarot reader, mystic, or spiritual guide, though he had consulted many on his quest to find Carcosa. But what he felt now he guessed might be "aura", for he couldn't say with what sense he detected a presence on the other side, only that he did, and that's its power terrified him. He was like a shipwrecked sailor finding an island out to sea, rejoicing for safety, only, when standing on the isle, to feel it shudder and move beneath him, and to hear the colossal beat of a leviathan's heart.

Either side of the mighty door were two smaller ones, both ornately designed in their own way, though paling next to the central one, which had to lead to a throne-room of some kind. From the righthand door emerged a smartly dressed man in silk breaches and a tunic. He wore a jaunty hat on his head from which a feather emerged flamboyantly. He seemed to be trying to embody both Fool and nobleman simultaneously.

"Greetings, your Royal Highness," he said unctuously, bowing low before Cali with one leg extended forward. "The Princess Cassilda is busy, at the moment, and so she bids you await her pleasure."

Cali snarled.

"The matter is quite urgent, Eric."

The jester's shit-eating grin sent chills down Alan's spine.

"I'm sure it is, your Highness. But Cassilda is in the midst of difficult work—"

"She has never done a day of work in her life," Cali muttered. "But very well, will you show us to the dining hall and have food prepared? I am famished, and no doubt my companions feel the same way."

Alan had not noticed—too caught up in the wonders of the city—but his belly was growling, and his lips were parched.

"Very good," Eric said, bowing again. He led them through the lefthand door into a dining room lined with eerie portraits. Unlike the austere portraits that hung in English manors, these were impressionistic, taking their subjects and warping them beyond recognition, splicing their features with those of animals, imbedding landscapes into the contours of their bodies. Some of them were revoltingly intimate. Others, abstract to the point of obscurity.

A long black table occupied the centre of the room, but it only rose to mid-shin height. Cali showed the way by sitting cross-legged at the head of the table. Petruccio sat to her left, setting his tabla down beside him. Alan sat to her right. Though he had practiced yoga and been to many esoteric retreats, he could not ever remember eating a full meal sat like this.

"Cassilda will be with you," Eric said. "I shall have the finest disberries brought to you."

With that, the courtier departed.

"Though her courtesy may be lacking, my sister will see us," Cali said.

Alan took a deep breath, summoning his courage.

"Why are we here?"

It was such a simple question, yet it left the room ringing. He knew why *he* was here. It had been his life's work up to this point to find Carcosa, and now he intended to drink all of its delicacies. But it was clear Cali had another motive. She had been keen to take him to the palace and bring him before her sister right from the start. Why? He had been so caught up in the city's magic he had not paused to consider what lay beneath the surface. Thus far, he had not paid Cali for showing him the way into Carcosa, and so it seemed likely she would ask for a favour. But what kind of favour could he perform? One-handed, ignorant of the city's ways, what kind of service could he provide? His heart stumbled with misgivings.

Cali regarded him intently. There was an arctic coldness in her stare that seemed incongruous with the sensuality of the Ritual they had performed together. Suddenly, the ice seemed to break, and she smiled, reaching out and placing a hand on Alan's own. Her touch was electric, warm. Her fingers stroked his knuckles.

"Alan, you are right to question. I admit, I was excited, and in my excitement I forgot to explain everything to you . . . Firstly, are you grateful that you are finally a subject of Carcosa?"

"Yes!" Alan answered, perhaps a little too quickly. "Oh yes, never doubt it!"

"Good," Cali said, with a soft smirk. "You went through much to get here." She let go of his good hand and moved to the stump, stroking it briefly. There was a delicious fizzle of pain that seemed bizarrely connected with his crotch. "You have no doubt guessed that I wish to ask a favour of you, in return for bringing you here."

THE CLAW OF CRAVING

"Whatever it is, I'll do it," Alan whispered. He meant it with every fibre of his being. How could he deny the one who had given him the solution to his miserable life, the answer to the riddle?

He saw, out of the corner of his eye, Petruccio shaking his head. Was it a warning? Disbelief? Did Cali's seductive powers not work upon him? Alan's internal questions were silenced by Cali's smile. She raised her hand to his chin, thumb and index lightly gripping it, regarding him the way an Empress might regard her favourite lion.

"You will be my champion, in time."

Several courtiers entered, carrying large silver plates. Large white and orange fruits were stacked upon the plates: disberries. Alan's stomach churned at the sight of them. They were about the size of satsumas, therefore the word "berry" did not seem apt. However, like berries, it seems they grew prolifically upon a single stem. Their outer flesh formed screaming faces, so that the disberry plates looked like a stack of shrunken heads.

"These aren't . . . actual people?" Alan asked.

Cali laughed.

"No. No-one is quite certain why they grow this way. Perhaps it is to dissuade predators? Though I suppose that is a very Darwinian view of things."

Alan frowned.

"Forgive me, but I'm surprised you have heard of Darwin."

"They know a lot more about us than we do about them," Petruccio said. He took a disberry and bit into it ferociously. Orange pulp and juice ran down his chin. He wiped it with the back of one hand and smacked his lips. "Nothing beats the taste."

"Try one, Alan," Cali said.

He took a disberry, half expecting the face to start shrieking at him in protest. The face remained still and silent, though its expression was so potent that even static it exerted a kind of power. If it was a Darwinian defence mechanism, he couldn't doubt it was effective. He turned the disberry around so that he did not have to look at the face, then bit into it.

The sweetness nearly made him gag. Neither honey nor sugar could compare. But there was something else too, something fermented and alcoholic. He bit greedily again and Petruccio and Cali both laughed.

"Welcome to your new addiction, Alan," Petruccio said, with an orangey grin.

"Yes!" Alan said, barely taking breaths between bites. Eventually, he ate through to a core of black seeds. He imitated Cali and Petruccio and discarded this on his plate.

More courtiers appeared, these ones bringing goblets and wine. It was the spiciest wine Alan had ever tasted, to the extent he begged for water. They brought him a cup of clear liquid. When he sipped it, it was salty.

"Is this sea water?" he spluttered.

"What you're tasting isn't salt," Cali said. "It's grief."

"Grief?"

"Yes. The waters of Carcosa are full of lamentation."

Despite the saltiness, or "grief", the water did quench his first. His second trial of the wine was more cautious and successful.

"What gives it that spice?" A joke occurred to him. "Anger?"

Cali looked at him seriously, then a smile spread across her perfect lips.

"Desire," she replied, and drank deeply. He watched the gentle undulations of her slender neck as she swallowed and swallowed and swallowed . . .

Eric returned to them.

"Princess Cassilda will see you now."

Eric led them back into the hallway with the three doors, and then through the righthand entrance from which he had originally appeared. They found themselves in a vast courtroom, ornamented with pillars, and bare of any portraits or artwork. It was a dusty place, the kind of room Alan would have thought had been long abandoned, had he not seen evidence to the contrary. Two large windows emitted a ghostly glow. Shadows brooded in the corners, avoiding the light.

From the darkness emerged a pale woman.

The real Cassilda was quite unlike her stage version, who had been a more conventional beauty. Her looks instantly struck Alan's soul, though not entirely in a pleasant way. Her hair was a cascade of filigreed gold, pale to the point of yellowness. Her flesh was white as cocaine. Her eyes were so heavily shadowed they were almost corpse-like, yet the pupils glittered, gold with flecks of ruby. Her every feature was painfully delicate, the nose a brushstroke of albescent paint, her lips a pale purple smudge, her cheeks a beautiful angularity like the outline of ornate furniture beneath a white sheet. She wore a bridal dress, but it seemed grey compared to her albino flesh. Her body was waif-thin, skeletal. She looked close to disappearing. And the sorrow of her gaze was a crippling mantle for anyone to endure.

"Sister," Cali said, softly.

Cassilda regarded Cali; in every way the sisters were opposite. Cali, black-fleshed and voluptuous. Cassilda, a pale wraith of ethereal beauty.

"Thou look'st like a common busker, begging for coin . . . " Cassilda remarked, eyeing Cali's instrument, still slung over her back. Her golden eyes fixed on Alan. "And thou hast brought *another* one, sister?"

Alan felt his fist clench. He resented being thought of as merely one of a crowd, one no different to the long line who came before. To be thought of as *ordinary*, after all he had endured as a result of his strangeness, after all he'd had to give up, was intolerable.

"You know as well as I, sister, that Carcosa's deliverance must come from outside. We are too set in our ways."

"Deliverance?" Alan said.

"Dare'st thou *speak* in the presence of royalty?" Cassilda snapped, her outrage only just managing to elevate her depressive monotone above conversational volume.

"This is precisely what I mean, *dear* sister," Cali said, through gritted teeth. "It is time we did away with such pointless formalities. Perhaps fewer soldiers would have died in the siege had we not stuck to such antiquated notions of warfare?"

Cassilda's dead eyes conveyed a glacial wrath.

"Dost thou accuse me of expending lives? What of the lives thou could have saved were'st thou *here* sister?"

Cali paled with rage.

Alan opened his mouth and Petruccio kicked him. Alan shot him a look and the dwarf shook his head, advising him to stay out of it.

Cali, however, had recovered herself. She took a deep breath.

"Sister, we disagree on many things, but I think we *can* agree on one thing: we must be ready for when the Pe'karians return."

Cassilda snorted. She turned away from Cali, pacing back and forth across the dark room.

"There's something unknown to thee, sister. I'm almost afraid to tell thee."

"What is it?" Cali sounded breathless, a rare condition for one so powerful.

Cassilda turned, fixing her twin with an expression so terribly hopeless it was all Alan could do not to fall to his knees and bash his head against the floor.

"They have taken Mother."

A choking sound escaped Cali's lips.

"Impossible . . . "

Cassilda shook her head.

"No, sister. Assassins came. Armed with magics. They took her in the night."

"What of Father? Why did He not stop them?"

"He sleeps," Cassilda said, gravely.

"Sleeps?" Alan exclaimed, his credulity stretched.

"When you are the age of the universe, you too shall know the joy of sleep," Cali said. Her face, however, showed no levity. There was a grief in her eyes deeper than a black hole.

"Thou should'st have been here, sister," Cassilda said, a soft savagery in her voice. "Thy power could have stopped them. Instead, thou were't debasing yourself with this *pervert*." She pointed at Alan.

Cali, normally so ferocious, had no response—grief had blown out the flame of her tenacity.

Alan found the words instead.

"If I am partly the cause of this tragedy, then let me make amends. You say she was captured, not killed?"

Cassilda's gaze fell on Alan, at last granting him personhood. He could tell she was furious at his outburst, but also a little intrigued by how boldly he continued to interrupt.

"Who art thou, then? What skills dost thou have that will allow thee to contend with the demons of Pe'kar, warriors so savage they slew ten thousand of our men in a single battle and defiled the corpses of each and every one."

Alan swallowed.

Cassilda's eyes alighted on his stump.

"And thou art a cripple, too, I see? How glorious, sister! Shall I kiss the feet of our *saviour*?"

Cali snarled.

"Let him speak."

Alan hesitated, looking between the two women, each terrifying in their own way. Cali seemed to be egging him on. He could feel she was pleased with his offer to help.

"When I came here, I thought that my journey was over . . . " he began. "But now I realise I must have come here for a reason. I believe that reason has now been made clear. I will help save your mother."

To his horror, Cassilda laughed. It was a surprisingly full and deep sound, the laugh of a grimy innkeeper after a hard day's work, too loud and boisterous to come out of a waif.

"What a speech!" she said, clapping her hands together. "Dost thou think that because I speak in the high tongue, that my speech is formal, that I will be swayed by pretty words? What nonsense hast my sister filled thy head with?"

"It is not nonsense, Cassilda," Cali said, firmly. "He is right. We do not have the soldiers to spare. Would you leave the city undefended? We must do as they did: send a small party, more difficult to detect, and win her back with stealth and guile." Cali sighed deeply. "Too many of our greatest fell in the last battle, sister. You know this. I had intended to recruit those with *different* minds, that we might have new soldiers for the war." Cali looked at Alan sadly. "I'd hoped you might have time to train and prepare before your first venture, but it seems circumstance compels action now."

Alan made sure to keep his face neutral, but he could not help but feel there was something *performative* in her words, as though she were saying this for the benefit of unseen listeners. He would not have noticed it had he not so recently observed the mummers performing their play, but his brain had become acutely aware of the subtle distinction between natural and theatrical speech. Cali was not being entirely honest, though in what way, he could not be certain. He was sure she would explain all when they were alone again.

The thought of being alone with her nearly distracted him from Cassilda's question.

"Thou hast not answered me," she said, imperiously. "What skills dost thou have? What is so special about this one-handed miscreant from Urth?"

Alan found he could not answer.

Cassilda sneered. Her petite face wore the expression particularly cruelly.

"This seems to me delusion and fantasy."

"Sister!" Cali said, and the authority in her voice shook the room. "I tire of your mockery. What harm can it do to send a party to rescue Mother? What would you do, sit here and grieve, like you have done for your entire life?"

Cassilda snarled.

"Do not speak to me like that!" And for a moment, she resembled Cali as she had in the market, berating Alan for the folly of his assumption that the palaces of imagination were fallen. Her hair shone white as starlight, her eyes turned black as coals, gleaming darkly. Her entire body radiated a tangible darkness—a black wrath that terrified him. Petruccio averted his eyes. Only Cali stood firm, gritting her teeth as though to form a barrier against her sister's rage. Then the moment passed, and Cassilda was herself again, so slight as to be moved by a gust of wind, or so she seemed.

"Forgive my anger, Cali," Cassilda muttered. "Thou art right. I have wasted long millennia weeping for no good reason." Her golden eyes rose and locked with Cali's. "And that is why I am coming with thee."

Cali looked like she had been slapped.

"No, sister, you should not—I didn't mean—"

"I will hear no argument," Cassilda said, surprising steel in her voice. "I will journey with thee to Pe'kar, and use whatever power lies within my blood to save Mother."

"But who will govern Carcosa in your stead, sister? You are needed here."

Cassilda waved a hand.

"Eric may seem a fool, but he is very diligent in matters of state, and exceedingly loyal. If matters grow dire, Father will wake; he always does. Besides, thou know'st as well as I do, sister, that Carcosa is a law unto itself."

Cali looked like she wanted to refuse with all her heart, but finally she nodded.

"Very well. But we shall not be going to land of Blue Light immediately."

Cassilda cocked her head.

"Why not?"

"You are the keeper of the old ways, sister. And so, I think you will like what I have in mind." Cali smiled at Alan. "In Yhtill, there is a weapon of great power, once wielded by the great warrior Haercus, in a time ancient even to our Father."

THE CLAW OF CRAVING

Cassilda's eyes widened, giving her the impression of a young girl—a terrible illusion, given she was older than civilisation on Earth (or "Urth" as she had called it).

"The Claw!"

"Yes," Cali said. "It may only be wielded by a one-handed warrior. Alan now qualifies. We have been too fair and honourable in our fight with the demon imposter, Pe'kar. We should even the odds, summon the ancient technologies of our forbearers, and put an end to this war."

Cassilda smiled. Alan could not help but think of the sun rising over a frosted field.

"I hate speeches, but it was well said, sister."

The two shared a brief moment—no hugs, handshakes, or kisses—but Alan could tell a rift had been temporarily healed.

"To Yhtill, then," Cali said. "Where you, Alan, will be made whole."

CHAPTER 9:

ONE MORE FOR THE ROAD

EXTENSIVE PROVISIONS WERE PACKED. The palace of Carcosa spared no expense outfitting them for the adventure. Bags filled with disberries, water, wine, bread, meat, and other exotic foods were loaded onto creatures called *quinels* that loosely resembled camels, save that they had five legs, a middle one descending from the belly down to the ground and offering them a kind of additional support. Petruccio explained they used this to probe the ground for potential quicksand or quagmire. There were given two of these creatures for carrying supplies.

They were also provided with fresh clothing for the journey. Alan was gifted a pair of beautiful, black-leather shoes for his blistered feet. Petruccio was given a walking stick. Cassilda and Cali both were outfitted with burqa-like garments that hid their royalty from prying eyes. These veils were spun from the thread of chameleon worms, so Cali told Alan, and could change hue depending on the environment. They would dispense with them once a few miles from Carcosa, for they were restrictive to movement. However, they would no doubt come in handy later on.

It was strange to Alan, departing Carcosa. He had only just arrived. They had spent perhaps three quarters of a day there. The sky was back now, lit only by stars and the half-devoured moon. He promised himself he would return and plumb its secrets.

The guards let them out of the city without issue. Just outside the main gate, they met someone they did not expect.

LeBarron waited, bowing low before the two women. Alan wondered how he knew who was behind the veils, but then again, perhaps he and Petruccio were the giveaways.

"I bid thee not impede us, mummer," Cassilda said. "Lest I have to order your execution."

LeBarron bowed low once again.

"Forgive me, noble princess. I do not come to impede, but to aid."

"Aid? What possible aid could thou give?"

"I am skilled with a sword." Indeed, he had a short scimitar sheathed at his hip. "And should you need entertainment for the road to alleviate the boredom of long hours walking . . . " At this, his eyes unmistakably flitted to Cali. "Then I know a number of plays by heart."

"Let him join us, sister. I see no harm. If he is a nuisance, you may kill him."

"He is a servant of The Stranger."

"Exactly. His skills might prove useful."

"He cannot be trusted," Cassilda said, her voice haughty and aggravated.

"He is a servant of The Stranger, not The Stranger himself."

To Alan's surprise, Cassilda turned to him.

"And what dost thou think, pervert of Urth? Dost thou think we should take this braggart into our party?"

Alan looked at LeBarron. The man was a rogue, but he had known Alan's name, and seemed to know things about the world opaque even to Cali and Petruccio.

"I think we should."

Cassilda sighed.

"Very well."

LeBarron thanked them graciously and bowed a third time. When he straightened, he winked at Alan.

They journeyed across the desert, led by Cali. According to her, they were heading north, though Alan wondered whether north had a different meaning in this strange land. After a mile or so, the two royal sisters discarded their magical veils. Cali donned a suit of armour similar to the ones worn by the guards, though it had less plates, and therefore greater mobility. The slabs of spiked chitin were joined by leather strips. Alan did not need convincing she was a fearsome warrior.

Cassilda wore her bridal dress. Alan had opened his mouth to question its practicality, but Cali and Petruccio had both shot him a warning look, and he'd closed his mouth again. The bridal train trailed in the sand, but otherwise she seemed relatively comfortable.

The quinels snorted and whinnied.

After many hours of walking, Alan took his first sight of Hali. The Black Lake was bigger than Loch Lomond, an expanse so vast it reached the horizon and continued beyond it. Its face was a perfect mirror-sheen, unnaturally still and flat despite the ever-blusterous winds. Yellow flowers, the size of small elephants, blossomed on its surface, poisonous lilies upon a pond large as an ocean. The sense of scale conveyed the impression that Alan had actually shrunk. He could imagine, with horror, a colossal dragonfly swooping overhead and him but a newt struggling to escape detection.

"We will circumnavigate the lake," Cali said. "On the far side, Hali bleeds into the soil, creating the marshes we know as Yhtill."

They went only a little further before deciding to rest.

A few lustless trees grew by the side of the lake. These Petruccio cut down with a one-handed axe. Soon, they had a fire going, sparked into life by twisting a piece of wood between flat palms while it rested on another, the friction generating heat and then flame. Alan was not much of an outdoorsman, and so he wondered at the skill and ease with which Petruccio did all this. A man of many talents, it seemed: a musician, an artist, and a survivalist.

The wood burned bright yellow, emitting a sulphurous smog into the sky.

"Don't inhale too deeply," the dwarf warned, as Alan sat down by the fire, extending his bare feet towards the warmth.

"You will be dreaming of eidolons and demons," LeBarron added, laughing. He plumped down next to Alan. As the firelight played across his face, every flicker seemed to reveal a new person.

"I would prefer thou avoided talk of demons while we lie beyond the walls of my Father's city," Cassilda said. She had also settled by the fire, sitting in the traditional posture of a royal woman, with legs to one side, her back straight.

LeBarron held up his hands, *mea culpa*.

"Let us not allow superstition to override our courage, sister," Cali remarked. She sat cross-legged, completing their strange circle.

"Perhaps thou art right," Cassilda said, loftily. Her eyes never left the flame. There was something unmistakeably enchanting about her; melancholy, which in others was mopey and draining, was a siren song for her. "If Pe'kar is a demon, then our thoughts give him power."

Cali made no reply. Now she, too, was fixated upon the fire. Alan wondered what thoughts ran through her head.

One by one, the group fell asleep. Cali and Cassilda were first. Then LeBarron turned in, resting the back of his head against the rump of one of the quinels.

Alan could not sleep, however. It was still technically his first night in Carcosa—no, that was not quite right, for Carcosa was the city not the world it inhabited, he would have to ask someone about that—and his body and mind fomented with energy. A welter of thoughts and feelings threatened to envelop him in mania. He fought continually to stave it off and still his mind, but always it excited itself again to frenzy. He would never sleep like this. He could hardly sit still, let alone let go of consciousness.

Petruccio, it seemed, also had no desire to sleep.

"You painted those images, in *The Black Star*," Alan said, suddenly.

Petruccio nodded.

"Why did you say I was not ready to know who did them?"

"You weren't. You would have asked me a thousand irrelevant questions. The only way for you to understand was to see this place for yourself." Petruccio sighed. "I regard those paintings as failures, to be honest, though Cali is fond of them."

"They were hauntingly beautiful."

"That is kind, but they fail in their purpose, which is to capture the *essence* of Carcosa."

Alan frowned.

"Can any painting capture the essence of something?"

"Of course it can," Petruccio replied. "Portraits rarely look *exactly* like their subjects, do they? We invented cameras for that purpose—though even they can be treacherous. Only a shallow rendering. The purpose of a painting is to capture the inner soul of the subject, to describe something evident only to the secret senses."

"You are clearly a deep artist."

"This world has given me more time than most to contemplate these questions, though I am still a novice in the eyes of the elite. That will change once I find the pigment, however."

"Pigment?"

"You have no doubt heard the phrase that a workman is only as good as their tools? I have taken that a little to heart, perhaps. There is a legend—isn't there always?—of a great artist who lived in the time of Haercus, called Uboth. He distilled a pigment from his own dreams: the *oneiric pigment*. Imagine that! To paint with dream-stuff! It was said that whatever he painted came alive, and that is how Carcosa was built."

Alan's breath shortened.

"It was *painted* into being?"

Petruccio nodded.

"How else could it have been born? No stonemason could have constructed it. The legend continues that Uboth began to fear what his pigment could be used for, so he hid it away—he was not capable of destroying it. Whoever finds this pigment could paint entire worlds into being. They could remap the night sky, raise cities, create worlds within worlds . . . That is what I seek."

"And Cali supports you in this?"

Petruccio smiled, sadly.

"She knows I will go mad if I do not try."

Alan nodded.

"I understand that feeling."

Petruccio stared at him.

"Perhaps you do. Maybe more than anyone else here. I had not considered that."

Alan swallowed. He could feel truths bubbling up his throat; they had to be spilled, or else he would choke.

"When I was a boy, about six, my mother—Alyssa—and my father—Aaron—they found me digging in their garden. Mother was house proud, so you can imagine her rage."

Petruccio chuckled.

"I had dug fully three feet deep, upheaved flower beds, destroyed the evenly cut grass. There was a pile of dirt and worms beside the hole I'd dug. When they asked me what I was doing, I told them I was digging for gold."

Alan felt a well of emotion then thinking of his parents, whom he would likely never see again. Even though they had slammed the door in his face, he still missed them, still felt as though he had failed them, and not the other way around.

"They were angry, but they understood," he continued. "I was a kid. I had no doubt watched some pirate-show or adventure program. They filled in the hole and tried to forgive me."

Petruccio smiled darkly.

"But you weren't done?"

Alan shook his head.

"No. I crept out of the house in the middle of the night. I began to dig again. I wasn't digging for gold, you see. I was digging because I knew, at some point, I would fall through the world. I had to know how deep the illusion went. I had to know . . . "

Alan realised he was crying. If Petruccio judged him, he gave no sign.

"What awoke the curiosity within you? You were only six when this happened. That is a young age to begin questioning the world."

"I thought that coming here would answer that question," Alan said.

"But instead, you only have more questions?"

Alan laughed, tears still running down his face. Petruccio laughed with him.

"You are an interesting man, Alan Chambers. I think you have been thoroughly misjudged."

"By who?"

Petruccio frowned, as though the answer were obvious.

"By the universe." He sighed. "You should rest. I will keep watch for the first part of the night."

Alan nodded. The nervous energy had finally dissipated from his limbs. He felt he could sleep. He lay down upon a blanket laid over the soft sand, it was not a bad bed at all. He closed his eyes, and soon the crackling of the fire lulled him into oblivion.

He awoke what felt like seconds later, though no doubt was many hours. He had been stirred by some movement; not sinister, simply enough to rouse him from slumber. Petruccio lay on his side, fast asleep. Alan saw Cali and LeBarron stood by the fire. They were talking softly, too softly for his sleep-addled brain to discern meaning.

Quietly, the two turned and set off into the darkness.

As suddenly as if he had been splashed with water, he was fully awake. *Where are they going? What are they doing?* Were they plotting against the group?

He waited several agonising seconds, then slowly rose from his own bed. He felt guilty leaving the sleeping Cassilda by the fire—

what if they were ambushed?—but he considered that she was likely more powerful than she seemed, gifted like her sister with magical abilities.

Cali and LeBarron walked purposefully towards a little copse of trees on the edge of Hali's waters. The moon was largely obscured by clouds that looked as though they had caught the plague, pustulous and yellowing. Still, though it was dark, Alan trod softly, and kept to the shadows.

The trees formed a thicket, romantically lit by starlight, the water lapping at the tree roots. Alan dared not approach too close, for fear of being discovered, but he was close enough now that he might overhear their secret conversation.

There was no conversation, however. Cali removed the silken garment she had slept in, letting it slip to her feet, revealing her gorgeous body—a woman of shadow incarnate. Alan's heart quickened. This was no traitor's council, but a tryst, and he was now the voyeur watching. Cassilda's mocking accusation came back to him: *pervert*.

But he could not draw his eyes away.

Cali and LeBarron's lips met. His hands went to her waist, then lower, cupping her muscular buttocks. Alan watched their tongues dance in starlight. His heart beat so loud he was sure it would give him away. He lay flat upon the ground, his cock painfully pressing against the sand, but he dared not move for fear of discovery.

"Who would you like me to be, Princess?" LeBarron murmured.

"Be no-one."

Cali stepped back from LeBarron, slowly kneeling, her serpent's eyes gazing up at him, biting her lip, the ultimate tease. She stroked his chest as she did so. He was wearing a white shirt, but he hastily unbuttoned it and threw it to one side, revealing an enviable physique. Her hands went to his trousers, unknotting the drawstring dextrously, then pulling them down. He stepped free of the clothes and his enormous cock rose to meet her.

Cali smiled, evidently pleased.

She placed one hand around the shaft, her fingers almost failing to fully wrap around its thickness—Alan remembered how she had pleasured him during the first stage of the Ritual of Five. But had that merely been perfunctory for her? Had he mistaken ritual for reality? Tears threatened again. Perhaps that was Alan's ultimate flaw? He had spent his life unable to discern fact from fiction, and thus he had been led to the shores of an imaginary world. *And even here, you cannot see the truth,* a cruel voice said.

Cali ran her tongue around the tip of LeBarron's penis. Her tongue extended, reaching the impossible length Alan had felt when she penetrated him, and looped about the shaft. Then, she withdrew her tongue, leaving his member coated in glistening saliva.

"My role demands many sexual acts," Cali purred. "But this I only do for those I truly desire."

"I'm honoured," LeBarron said, with a trace of mockery.

"You will be."

Slowly, Cali put her lips around LeBarron's cock. Alan noted, with agonising arousal and also painful self-criticism, how her lips had to stretch to fit even the tip of his hugeness in her mouth. He filled her up, her jaw opened as wide as it could. She emitted a low moaning sound, then pushed deeper. At halfway down his massive length, it seemed she could go no farther. She began to gently nod, pushing him deeper into her throat. LeBarron let out a groan of pleasure.

While ministering to him with her beautiful mouth, she began to stroke with one hand, then—again, to Alan's intense jealousy—with two.

"Yes," LeBarron said. "Yes!"

Finally, after minutes that seemed hours to the tortured Alan, she withdrew her lips, a trail of glistening saliva still linking LeBarron and her.

"I want—" he began.

"Yes," Cali answered, reading his intention. She untucked her legs and rolled over onto her front, lying in a sphinx-like posture, the way one would when preparing to receive a massage. Her huge breasts spread against the ground. She lifted her hips toward LeBarron. He squatted over her in a horse stance, lowering his massive, glistening cock to her buttocks. He spread her cheeks aside and pushed into her.

Cali cried out, her face a mask of surprise and pleasure. She looked back at LeBarron with an expression of submissiveness that set Alan's whole body on fire—if only she could look at him that way! LeBarron grinned.

He began to push into her again, and Cali's loud moan sent a thrill through Alan he couldn't believe. He had never heard a woman show her pleasure so vocally. Did that mean he was a poor lover? Or was this mere theatre? It seemed real enough, but then, he had a problem deciphering reality, as he had come to realise.

LeBarron began gently, allowing Cali to acclimate to the size of him. The thought of what he was doing to her, *stretching her*, the way he had stretched her lips, was almost too much for Alan to bear. Yet at the same time he wished he could see.

Alan knew his thoughts were outrageously pornographic, but it was as Cassilda had said: he *was* a pervert at heart. This scene forced him to confront the graphic truth of that.

Soon, LeBarron began to remorselessly fuck Cali. The sound of his hips smacking against hers was strangely hypnotic, as was the ripple that passed through the flesh of her buttocks with each impact.

"You want me to stop holding back, Princess?"

"Yes!" Cali said. "Yes!" She sounded like she was pleading with him, and that made Alan's heart race so fast he felt dizzy. He needed to leave—if his sanity was going to survive—yet he could not.

LeBarron began thrust so hard and fast that Cali's back arched like a cat's, and she let out whimpering squeals. After a minute of solid thrusting she began to scream.

She cried out, her eyes squeezed tightly shut with pleasure. Alan realised he would have shot his load a long time ago, but LeBarron kept going, merciless, until Cali's squeals rose in pitch once more and she came for the second time.

With an effort of will like shaking off sleep paralysis, Alan began to crawl backwards, away from the thicket, away from the carnal acts within. The lovers were distracted and did not even notice as he finally rose to his feet and ran back to the campfire.

When he arrived, he found Cassilda awake. She was looking at him intently, her eyes penetrating the depths of his misery without effort.

"I see thou hast discovered my sister's true nature."

Alan sat by the fire. He was exhausted, as though he had run miles. His limbs were still trembling. Blood rushed through his veins so fast it seemed to have forgotten its role to bring oxygen and nutrients to his extremities.

"I . . . " Alan did not know what to say. He felt foolish, ashamed, unmanned, outraged, aroused, all these and more.

THE CLAW OF CRAVING

"She is a creature of her lusts, when all is said and done," Cassilda said. Her tone was soft. She sounded sympathetic, even. Perhaps Alan was not the first heart Cali had broken. "But thou art no fool for falling prey to her seductions. Few can resist."

Alan found his eyes wandering to the sleeping Petruccio.

"Those who can," Cassilda continued. "Are committed to great purpose. I wonder . . . what is thy purpose, Alan?"

It was the first time she had used his name.

"My purpose was to find Carcosa," he said. "But now I am here, I don't know. I hope that I can help save your mother."

Cassilda waved her hand, as though his words were airy nothings.

"Thou agreed to that because thou art infatuated with my sister," Cassilda said. "Or perhaps, if I were being generous, because thou hast a dutiful and selfless soul. That is not what you desire, and one's purpose always arises from some deep desire. I doubt thou will think of it now. But in time, search thyself, and it may reveal itself in all its splendour."

Humbled, Alan inclined his head.

"I thank you—thee—Princess Cassilda."

She smiled at his clumsy attempt at the formal speech.

"Perhaps The Claw is what I seek?" he said, after a few moments. "She said it would make me whole."

Cassilda shook her head.

"Nay. The Claw may give thee back thy lost hand, but it cannot make thee whole. That is only in *thy* power."

He contemplated her words.

"If it is not impertinent to ask . . . " Alan stammered with nerves. "I am curious: why do you wear a bridal gown?"

He feared, for a moment, he had overstepped. Cassilda seemed to glow with a deadly moonlight. Then, she softened, her delicate features portraying the petulant beauty of drooping flowers.

"I was betrothed, long ago. Too long ago, though it seems yesterday."

"To The Stranger?" Alan said, cottoning on. He realised he had seen the drama performed in LeBarron's play, which he now viewed in a very different light, given what he had just witnessed.

Cassilda nodded.

"Yes. And oh, he was beautiful . . . like thou canst not dream, Alan. A being of pure and formless wonder! And his face!" She

66

hissed at this, as though suddenly beholding it in the flame, as vivid as the day she had last looked upon it. "On the eve of our wedding, before we had sworn our sacred vows, he came to my chambers . . . r-r-ra . . . " Silver tears fell from Cassilda's eyes. It was only then he realised how large her eyes were, windows into a vast soul. She seemed, if possible, even more delicate and beautiful as she wept. " . . . It was against my will," she finished, not able to use the other word. "And then he vanished. No one has seen him. His followers prophesy his return, that one day the True Stranger shall come again to Carcosa, seeking his bride." Cassilda showed her teeth, feral as a wolf. "But he shall not have her!"

"I'm . . . sorry," Alan said.

"Do not be sorry, Alan." She dried her tears with the hem of her dress. "Thou art unlike him, or *him*." She jerked her head in the direction of the glade, where even now Cali and LeBarron would still be entwined—how Alan hated and envied and desired them, all at once. "Better, by far. I heard thee talking with Petruccio. Thou hast been looking for something thy whole life, but it is not Carcosa. It is within thyself. When thou hast found it, thou will know. And in answer to thy question, this dress is a reminder to me, perhaps one that I grow out of, of the error of trust."

It seemed, at that moment, she awakened, as though this entire discourse she had been dream-speaking. She looked at Alan with the alacrity of a hawk.

"I say too much," she muttered. "Goodnight."

She threw herself down upon her blanket.

Alan remained by the fire, stunned. He had never experienced such a range of emotions in one evening. As an eternal seeker of experience, he could not write it off as a bad thing. He heard Cali and LeBarron's footsteps approaching and, for some reason unknown to him, decided to conceal his knowledge of their act a little longer. He likewise threw himself down on the blanket and closed his eyes, imitating sleep.

He could not, however, prevent a soft smile from curling his lips.

Who was the actor now?

CHAPTER 10:
THE MARSHES

I T TOOK THEM five days to skirt Lake Hali's shores
to the northern side. During that journey, Alan saw
increasingly strange things.

Lake Hali's banks were swarmed by the same spine-sailed
lizards he'd seen lazing on the steps leading up to the palace. They
eyed the quinels with a hunger that bordered on lascivious.

"Dimetrodons," Petruccio said. "Or at least that's what I call
them—if you know your palaeontology. Best give them a wide
berth. They prefer hunting reptiles and amphibians, but given the
chance, they'll go for something with two legs."

Though Alan heeded Petruccio's warning, and the entire party
kept their distance from the lake's shores, he could not help but
find enchantment in these creatures; there was a strange beauty to
them, especially as the twin suns set over Hali, turning their
curiously ornamental sails into stained-glass windows: purples,
reds, violets, greens, and of course yellows that wounded the eye.
It seemed to Alan the dimetrodons sought the sunlight upon their
sails. Perhaps it was mere thermoregulation. Yet, there was a
knowing in their eyes, as if they put on this curious display for him.
LeBarron's words returned to Alan in these moments: *We are all
The Stranger in His many guises.* Did that include beasts too?

The strangeness, however, was only just beginning.

Reaching the northern shore of Hali, they began to venture into
the marshlands in earnest. Alan noticed the shifting of the
landscape. The sand became a watery gruel. Hali's tributaries
formed a spiderweb of black, gushing rivers that produced
scattered islands. Once, Alan accidentally slipped and dunked his
foot into the waters. The same cold that had assailed him in the

second stage of the Ritual brought icy nerve-death to his toes. He quickly withdrew his leg. He'd passed the trial once and felt no need to prove himself again. From there on, he was far more careful, avoiding the water wherever possible.

The flora and fauna, too, changed. Gone were the spindly trees that had hugged the lake's banks. Here, the trees were thick, tall, coniferous, like hairy limbs rising out of the ground to grapple the sky. There was no canopy to speak of, creating a curious sense of vastness. He saw not one flower. Instead, mushrooms bloomed from every orifice in soil and sapling.

Petruccio's comment about palaeontology rang in Alan's head, and he realised that the landscape he was looking at reminded him of a TV program he'd watched as a kid where they explored different eras of the Earth's pre-history, rendering the environments and creatures in what was probably now outdated CGI. Each episode focused on a different period: Triassic, Permian, Carboniferous . . . Each was separated by distances of time that seemed impossible, nonsensical. Their mention evoked nervous laughter. Three hundred million years ago? How could the human mind, with its mere span of threescore-and-ten, possibly contemplate that vast gulf? Let alone the things which dwelt in a time so primordial. Things that did not follow the rules of modern life on Earth. Things altogether stranger than fiction.

"Why would Haercus leave The Claw in such a place?" Alan found himself asking, on the seventh day. They had set up camp on a preciously rare patch of solid ground. Their fire seemed dismal and small, where in the desert it had wildly bloomed.

"For the same reason Uboth hid the pigment," Petruccio answered. "He feared its power, and feared others abusing that power."

"This had better be worth it," Alan said, ashamed of his uncharacteristic pessimism, but unable to repress it. The air was oppressively humid and wet. Every lungful felt like he was sluicing the inside of his airways with something profane.

"Alan has a point," Cassilda said, turning her sad, golden eyes on Cali. Over the last few days, Cassilda had torn the train from her bridal gown—sick of it trailing in Hali's waters—and made it into an ankle-length dress. It was still impractical, but improved. "Is this not wasted time? Mother hast been in the enemy's hands for over a week. What torments have we abandoned her to? What suffering—"

THE CLAW OF CRAVING

"Sister!" Cali said. "Do not allow panic to overwhelm your equilibrium."

Cassilda bit her lip, clearly wishing to respond, but deciding to keep the peace.

Cali softened, crouching by her sister and putting one arm around her shoulder.

"Mother is powerful. She will endure. We need The Claw, or else even our combined strength will not be enough to overcome the forces of Pe'kar. Besides . . . " Cali straitened. "From Yhtill, we will be able to sneak into the northern part of that cursed land."

"You have been to Pe'kar's lands before?" Alan asked.

"Regretfully, yes."

"What is—" But Alan's question was cut off as he leapt up, yowling. A disgusting creature had emerged from foliage. He hadn't seen it scuttling so close to the ground. Armour plates glinted in the wan light. Two antenna curved back from its head. There were no eyes. Rather, stigmata-like stalks protruded from its exoskeletal cranium. A millipede, but longer than a car.

"Stay back!" Petruccio said. "Arthropleura can spit cyanide!"

The quinels shrieked and moved to bolt, but Cassilda gripped their reins—had they fled, they would have been without equipment or food supplies.

The creature reared, reaching human eye-level, an affront to the supremacy of *homo sapiens. An affront to God,* Alan couldn't help but think, if indeed God existed in this strange domain. Its legs furiously undulated, as though with excited anticipation. Its mandibles snapped.

"Yah!"

Alan wheeled as a knight leapt in front of him and Petruccio. The knight's features were proud and wild-eyed, as though combat were a delightful sport to him. His blade flashed across the arthropleura's exposed underbelly and it hissed as ichorous blood spilled from the wound. It threw itself forward, attempting to flatten the gallant knight, but he neatly sidestepped, dancing, it seemed, more than fighting. He straddled the monstrous beast and drove his blade down. It pinged off the segmented plates. The creature began to snake forward on its myriad legs towards Cassilda, perhaps deeming her easier prey. The knight let out a roar and drove his blade down again, this time finding the gap between two exoskeletal plates. The creature let out a shriek, pinned. The frantic movement of its excessive limbs sent chills down Alan's spine. He clapped his hands to his ears. Insects should not be able to make any sound at all, let alone a shriek like that. The knight twisted his blade, left then right. When he finally removed it, the arthropleura collapsed, though its death-twitches made Alan uncertain it had truly been slain.

The knight straightened and stepped towards their party. His blade shone with black-green ooze. His face glistened with sweat from his daring exertion.

"Do not be afraid, intrepid travellers," he declaimed. "For the noble knight, Antinous, is here to protect you."

Cali clapped, slow and derisory.

"A fine performance, LeBarron."

Alan blinked. How had he not seen? LeBarron stood before them, all grinning swagger.

"I thought so too," he said, taking a bow.

Cali smirked. Did Alan read lust in her eyes? *Let it go,* a part of him said. But he could not. She had enflamed his senses.

"We must be more careful," Petruccio said, grounding them all. If he felt emasculated by LeBarron's heroism, he gave no sign. "Yhtill is full of such horrors. Indeed, we have only glimpsed the scummy surface of this pond. We should proceed with great haste and always keep weapons ready."

All accepted the artist's wisdom. LeBarron kept his sword drawn. Cassilda hiked up her dress, revealing a slender white leg, a bejewelled dagger strapped to the thigh. Cassilda saw Alan looking and he quickly averted his eyes. Knowing her story, how could he objectify her so?

Petruccio fetched his fire-axe from a saddlebag, and Cali took up her strange sitar-like instrument. He wondered whether she intended to use it like a mace, or whether the instrument's terrible musical power extended into this realm also.

Alan had no weapon, but it seemed he was exempt, given his crippled status.

Before they moved on, Alan investigated the arthropleura. He felt repulsed by every inch of it, but he had long learned the art of overcoming disgust and facing his fears. He wasn't brave, per se, but he could force himself to do things others couldn't. He'd wondered whether the arthropleura's meaty platemail was the material used by the warriors of Carcosa to forge their armour, but looking closely he now realised the plates were too *small,* especially for the chest-piece. A flutter of anxiety ran through him. That meant there was something *bigger* out there, *much* bigger.

Onward, they forged, and Petruccio's prophecy came true. Yhtill was alive with wonder and horrors living side by side, and some things incorporating both. A dragonfly passed over their heads the size of an elephant. The buzzing of its wings was as loud as a helicopter. The entire party threw themselves to the ground as it swooped. The air shrieked as its scything limbs slashed. Had they been standing, one of them might have lost their heads. Alan watched its supernaturally bright colours disappear into the sweltering fog of the horizon.

Hali's waters—though they were three days' walk from the lakeshore now—were no longer cool. Here, they were warming, to such an extent that some pools frothed and bubbled, and others emitted columns of white vapour. Strange creatures cleaved to these baths. One, a mound of white flesh with flappy, wing-like fins and a face so long and drawn it resembled a duckbilled platypus, regarded them without moving, its beady yellow eyes accusatory but also sorrowful, as though it knew its wretched condition, and envied their state of bliss. Its disgusting mass made it seem helplessly beached, but after a cloud of water-mist passed across Alan's field of vision, he no longer saw it there.

"Alan."

He turned and saw Cali had drawn close to his side. She'd slung her sitar across her back. She walked proudly, head held high and back straight, as though the terrors of Yhtill were beneath her. She was undeniably beautiful in feature and form, but he realised that much of her beauty also stemmed from the way she held herself, the aura she projected.

"You seem troubled," she said.

He looked at the ground, partly in shame of what he'd witnessed, a guilt for his voyeurism gnawing at him, and partly because he needed to watch his footing in this treacherous place. The quinels did much better with their fifth, probing limb.

"It's this marsh," he said, able to admit that much; it wasn't exactly false. "It's getting to me."

Something brushed his hand and he fought the urge to yelp, but it was only a kind of bamboo-like reed. He had seen hundreds of these on their journey. Petruccio had cut one and revealed they were hollow inside, containing water. The fact they had no discernible flowerhead made them look strangely stunted and incomplete. Everything here seemed prototype, as though the Creator had not yet worked out the ideal forms his works should take.

"Are there gods in Carcosa, Cali?" he said.

Cali smiled.

"Yes. The King, my father, is a god." Alan noticed she did not add the traditional praise afterward. "Some say The Stranger is a god. I know our friend LeBarron would agree." Alan's jaw and fists tightened; he forced them to unclench, a futile exercise. "Of course, some believe Pe'Kar is a god."

"But who or what created all this? In our world, there are many theories, some religious and some secular."

"It is the same here."

Alan sighed.

"I was afraid you would say that. I had hoped that a place as magical as this would be more . . . certain."

"Ah, but would it be magical, if it was certain?"

Alan smiled.

"I suppose not."

"I can tell you what I believe, for what it's worth."

Her face was earnest. The serpent-eyes hypnotised him once more. He realised he would likely believe whatever she told him, no matter how farfetched.

"I believe that Yhtill, and other places like it, show us the state of things before order. You have seen the variegated life here. It is chaos. It is mutiny against form." Somewhere, a creature howled so loudly that Alan's sternum vibrated. Through a pall of vapour he saw something winged descend and snatch up a wriggling insectoid. They vanished beyond smog. "Order and form only arrive when *we* arrive, Alan. Then, everything we look at starts to take on predictable shapes. Look at these quinels, for example. Are they not perfect beasts of burden with their humps, their spindly legs, and their equine shape? It is almost as if they were designed for our purposes."

Alan frowned.

"So what you're saying is . . . "

"The world is designing itself *for* us. Of course, we consciously shape our environment too, to a degree. We build cities behind stone walls." She smiled, as though there were some irony in this beyond Alan's comprehension. "We breed animals for various uses. We pull up weeds . . . But our conscious intervention cannot account for all of it. It cannot account for the quinel, for the horse, for the hali-tree that produces wood of perfect temperament to make spear-hafts, or the ore in the earth that allows us to shape metal. The world responds to our needs." She cast her eyes over the fetid marshes. "And where we do not tread, the world once more devolves into the chaos of its origins."

Alan was a little shaken.

"It is . . . a fascinating idea. I shall have to meditate upon it."

Cali stopped and took Alan's chin in one delicate finger, lifting his eyes to meet hers. She was taller than him, he realised, by about five inches. The Ritual had been such an esoteric experience, he had not been paying attention to such details. Similarly, the city had overawed him with its grandeur. But stood here, she towered over him, and it was thrilling.

"Bear it in mind, Alan Chambers. That the world is listening to what we *desire*." Her voice was a low, feline purr. "So, think long and hard about what you want, and perhaps, perhaps, the world might respond."

She smiled, white-teethed and mysterious, and left him there. Hope and confusion warred within him. Eventually, he hurried after the others, not wishing to be left behind in this stagnant wasteland.

CHAPTER 11:
THE ROSE

"UP AHEAD," LeBarron whispered. He crouched low behind one of the bamboo-like bushes. His eyes were narrowed in concentration. He now resembled a ranger drawn from the archetypes of literature. Indeed, his face had grown thick stubble giving him the weatherbeaten look of a man of the wilds. "Soldier-demons."

Alan struggled to discern what LeBarron had spied: the marsh-fog seemed to be growing thicker with each passing day, and the air shimmered with heat waves. He was drenched in sweat. His robes clung to him, wetted through and stinking. The others were little better off. Only Cali seemed immune to the marsh's assault.

"I see," Alan said.

A patrol, it seemed, of ragged soldiery—ten or eleven in number. They were anthropoid, but clearly not human. Or perhaps they had once been human, but certain mutations had warped their physiologies into new eidolons.

"Why are their skulls that shape?" Alan whispered.

"They call it Pe'Kar's blessing," Cali said, grimly. "Should they perform well in his eyes, they are granted his boons."

Alan failed to see how conical skulls were a boon, other than making their silhouettes imposing, but he was coming to realise the immense deficit of his understanding and so had to accept there was perhaps some strange purpose he had not deciphered.

"We should go around them," LeBarron said, still speaking huskily, like a woodsman on the scent.

"I agree," Cassilda chimed. "They art many, and we few."

"No," Cali hissed, and it seemed she burned with rage. "Not long ago these devils laid siege to our city, sister, or have you

75

forgotten? Think of the piles of dead. Think of the warriors who died to defend Carcosa's walls. We must avenge them."

For the second time, Alan discerned a slight note of *theatricality* in Cali's voice, as though these words were designed to produce a certain effect, not really uttered from the heart.

Cassilda opened her mouth to protest, but Cali took off running towards the soldiers.

"She is mad!" Petruccio said, but he had risen to his feet and brandished his axe. "Let us be quick, then, and take them in ambush."

LeBarron laughed and leapt forward, immediately stepping once more into the role of a heroic knight. Petruccio charged, moving with surprisingly rapid pace considering his short legs. Cassilda remained.

"I shall protect thee, Alan," she said softly. "For thou art unarmed and dismembered."

"I thank you, princess, but will our friends not need your help?"

Cassilda smiled.

"Behold my sister in her element . . . "

Cali had unslung her instrument from her shoulders and strode boldly towards the demonic soldiers. Now, Alan could see more clearly. The soldiers of Pe'kar were not only gifted with conical heads, but the contours and edges of their skulls were alarmingly prominent, almost as if the bone were trying to force its way out from underneath the skin. Their eyes were therefore sunken deep in their head, apelike. They had no noses, only serpentine slits. Strange horns covered their body, apparently breaking the skin to make themselves known.

What he'd taken to be armour from a distance was actually a kind of aberration of hardened flesh and scale and cartilage. They were naked, in other words, but sexless. Scars marred where genitals had once been. Their hip sockets and knees had taken on a distinctly insect bulbousness.

There was nothing tribal, nor primitive about the way they organised themselves, however. One carried a banner, emblazoned with a six-pointed star upon eye-watering cerulean. One carried an instrument that resembled a trumpet. And all bore curved blades, like cutlasses.

They cried out in alarm as Cali descended upon them. To Alan's surprise, they hesitated, despite vastly outnumbering her.

Perhaps they had heard legends of her prowess? Their faces, ugly as they were, contorted in confusion.

"Die!" Cali struck a single chord upon her sitar, and the sound was so harsh that Alan nearly dropped to the ground, his knees buckling.

The foremost soldier took the full brunt of the sound-wave and ruptured. Blood burst from his eyes and mouth. The scream that left his lips was all-too-human as he collapsed, blood running from every available orifice, his corpse twitching.

The others rallied and charged. Cali began to strike at the notes of her sitar. Though they were harsh—vibrations that gnawed at the back of the teeth, that shrilly lingered in the inner ear—they were not random, there was a *pattern* to the disorder that made it somehow more disturbing. With each note, soldiers collapsed, their insides journeying rapidly towards the light like startled parasites. One, closer to Cali than most, fully disgorged his entrails out of his mouth.

But even with her magical powers, she could not account for them all. Three soldiers had circled around and now swept down upon her from the flank.

The first died by an axe to the brain, hurled by Petruccio with expert precision.

LeBarron leapt at the other two. His sword glinted as it cut through the air. It lodged in the chest of his foe. LeBarron grimaced and tried to dislodge it, but it remained stuck, nestled in the folds of organic armour. The second soldier seized their chance and drove a blade into LeBarron's side.

The actor roared with pain. He ripped his sword from its fleshy mooring, killing the first Pe'karian soldier in the process, then spun, slashing open the throat of his assassin.

The second soldier dropped, head nearly rolling from his shoulders, his throat a crimson geyser.

LeBarron touched the wound in his side, his fingers coming away bloody. He forced a grin that not even his supernatural acting skills could make real. He was in deep pain.

Cali had finished off the rest of the party. One Pe'karian lay, guttering, not quite dead.

"Hold, Cali," Petruccio said, stepping over the corpse of the soldier he'd slain and retrieving his axe in the process. "We might question this one for information."

"No," Cali spat. "Filth must die." She stamped upon the demon's face, reducing its elongated skull to broken pottery, brains leaking out across the black mud.

Petruccio frowned.

"We could have learned the enemy's position!"

"From a footsoldier? Please, Petruccio, spare me your misplaced mercy."

The dwarf did not look happy about it, but he wiped his axe clean and fastened it to his belt.

"Friends," LeBarron said. He was white as a sheet and staggered slightly as he walked back to them. "Let us—"

He collapsed.

Cali let out a curse in a tongue Alan did not know. Cassilda and he approached the stricken LeBarron, who was trying to rise, but couldn't. His tunic—usually white—was almost entirely red. A shocking amount of blood had pooled beneath him and soaked his breaches.

"Let us see the wound," Cassilda said, gravely.

Alan did the honour, gently pulling the actor's shirt away. He had to fight to control his visceral reaction. He was not squeamish, but the wound in LeBarron's side was deep and gory, disgorging unholy volumes of blood.

"That bad?" LeBarron said, seeing Alan's face. Alan was amazed to see the actor manage a genuine smile. Clearly, as a man of the stage, he saw the comedy in tragedy, and vice-versa.

"I will heal him." Cali knelt by his side and positioned her instrument diagonally across her body. She began to pluck notes, harmonious and sweet. Alan had often heard it said music was healing, but now he witnessed the literal truth of it, as the wound began to close before his eyes.

LeBarron let out a sigh of relief.

Then he screamed.

The wound had opened on the other side of his body. Cali swore again, a confusion of harsh syllables Alan couldn't parse.

Once again, she worked the sweet melody, and once again the wound sealed, only to reopen, this time in his stomach, causing LeBarron to retch with disgust. By now he was filthily pale, and his breathing was ragged.

"Their blades must have been coated with Pe'kar's bile," Cali said. "It is a special poison, native to demons. His wounds will resist all magical treatment . . . "

LeBarron's eyes went wide with understanding. Terror was perhaps the first real emotion he had ever exhibited. His face was paler, if possible, than Cassilda's. This was no performance. He had lost an astonishing amount of blood, and more was streaming out of him through his trembling fingers every second.

"Am I . . . am I going to die?"

"No," Alan said, surprising them all. "We must do this the old-fashioned way. Petruccio, I need you to apply pressure to stop the bleeding. Use his shirt."

The dwarf picked up LeBarron's bloodsoaked shirt and pressed firmly on LeBarron's stomach. The actor howled in pain.

"Is there a darning kit in the saddlebags?"

"Yes," Cali replied, and she went to the quinels, returning a moment later with a small leather pouch containing needle and thread.

"I'm going to die . . . " LeBarron whimpered.

"LeBarron," Alan said, not sure how to stoke optimism, having never needed to learn a bedside manner. That was a sad thought: had he ever really cared for anyone? "Think of your courage! Think about how you leapt boldly at that millipede! You had no fear then. I *envied* your bravery."

"You think I'm brave?" LeBarron choked. He was laughing. Blood ran from the side of his mouth. "I'm *nothing,* Alan. Just smoke and mirrors. When one is a stranger even to oneself, it's easy to ignore fear. But death, death makes everything real . . . "

LeBarron shuddered once, then his head fell back. He had passed out.

Cali cursed again.

"Alan, what hast happened to him?" Cassilda said. "Is he dead?"

"No," Alan said. "He has lost too much blood. He's . . . he's gone into shock. We must perform a transfusion."

"Hah!" Petruccio cried. "You're mad."

"I dare do all that may become a man," Alan murmured. "Who dares do more is none. I will need your help, Petruccio. I only have one hand."

The dwarf sobered, nodding.

"But what if your blood types are incompatible?"

The dwarf knew something of the real world.

"I am O-negative," Alan said.

LeBarron's eyes had rolled up into his skull, his head lolling with ataxia. His flesh was so clammy that Alan thought it would turn into melted wax.

"Find me some of that bamboo. The thinnest stems you can."

"Hollowgrass?"

"Whatever it's called. Hurry!"

Petruccio dashed away.

"Cassilda—"

"Yes?"

"I shall need a sliver of your dress."

She cut off a thin strip using her dagger.

"Will this suffice?"

Alan bowed gratefully.

"How dost thou know how to do all this?" Cassilda inquired. "Wert thou a physician?"

"No," Alan said, calmly. "But a woman once saved my life."

Alan rolled up the sleeve of his right arm.

"Bind my bicep," he instructed.

Cassilda took the narrow sliver of bridal dress and wrapped it tightly about Alan's arm, tugging the ends several times. Alan's veins stood out in his forearm, like serpents roused to anger. Though Alan no longer had fingers on his right hand, he still felt the eerie sensation of blood no longer reaching the extremities—a phantom or perhaps sympathetic deadness.

Petruccio returned the next moment, bearing bundles of thin reeds.

"I brought all I could."

"Thank you. This will be messier than ideal. We also lack any alcohol to clean the wound properly . . . I need you to cut this reed diagonally at both ends, so that they're sharp, like you would if you were making a quill."

Petruccio nodded. He applied his axe to the task and soon had succeeded.

Meanwhile, Alan asked Cassilda to thread the needle for him. She did so expertly. Now for the grisly work of sewing up LeBarron's open stomach . . .

"Who was this woman that you speak of?" Cali asked. Did he detect a note of jealousy in her voice?

"She was . . . a prostitute," he said, wincing in sympathetic pain as he pushed the needle through the folds of LeBarron's flesh. "Can someone apply pressure? Thank you, Petruccio."

"I see."

"She was more than that." Alan said, more defensively than he intended. "Her name was Rose. She . . . she knew a lot of things. Things about Thelema and I Ching and . . . "

"Things you thought could lead you to Carcosa?" Cali said, not concealing her mockery.

"Yes." Alan's thread-work was far from neat, especially using his left hand. The flesh was slippery with blood, but he was beginning to draw the edges of the wound together. Whatever black incantation prevented the wound from being healed via magical means could not resist Alan's trembling, blood-soaked fingers. "One night, Rose called me and said she had to see me."

"A whore called you?" Petruccio said. "Now *that* is rare."

"I have already said she was more than that," Alan said, though without rancour. His concentration was such that anger was bleeding out of him with the same rapidity blood was flowing from LeBarron. Petruccio helped by applying pressure with LeBarron's shirt. "We were . . . exploring magic together. She said she had made a breakthrough. She invited me to participate. Of course, I went."

The final stitch sealed the wound like a grisly smile. That seemed fitting for LeBarron.

Now, Alan took the reed Petruccio had prepared and tested it against his own skin. The severed end of the hollowgrass was indeed sharp, and the firmness of the plant meant that he was able to break skin. However, it could also bend, which would prove useful for making the transfusion smoothly.

"And?" Cali said.

Alan realised he had the rapt attention of all three.

He leaned over LeBarron and used his right forearm to compress LeBarron's bicep. Then he drove the reed into his forearm. He had to be careful. He was not as well-practiced finding the median cubital vein on others as he was on himself. LeBarron's flesh was already bruising with the rough treatment.

Finally, he made contact, felt the snag. It was in.

"We began the ritual, which involved bloodletting, and drinking each other's fluids . . . " Alan felt suddenly disgusted with himself. What had he been thinking? Whoever found paradise through the perversions of a vampire? *But you did, Alan. All roads led you here.* "Halfway through, we were interrupted. Her pimp

81

misinterpreted what has happening, thought I was roughing her up. He did to me what those soldiers did to LeBarron."

"Stabbed you?" Petruccio said.

"I still have the scar."

Alan now took the other end of the reed and pushed it against his own forearm, The skin split, a single orb of blood welling, and he forced it deeper, digging for the vein. He was well practiced from various explorations with drugs over the years.

There! He had it. He watched the green stem of the plant begin to turn red as his blood flowed through the hollow. He swallowed, fighting down nausea, and looked at Petruccio. His was the easiest face to tell a story to. The granitic austerity of his features made him look like he was listening with every fibre of his being, and perhaps he was.

"They kicked me out on the street, but Rose didn't leave me." Alan felt tears threatening. "She took me back to her place. It turned out she'd had to fix up quite a few of her sisters over the years. She was resourceful—and kind." Alan trembled. He could feel his life draining out of him. As he poured his blood, the story couldn't help but pour out too. "I don't remember much, I was delirious with blood loss. In fact, at times I thought I was already dead. I drifted into a blackness so deep I could almost believe there was nothing beyond it . . . I was terrified, and there was nothing I could do about it." He took a deep breath. "But she stitched me up. She knew she couldn't take me to the police, there would be questions when they patched me up that would lead back to her pimp, and that would be the end of her. The end of me, too. So, she sat me down in a chair and got out her little medical kit." Tears scorched Alan's cheeks, hotter even than the warm blood against his arm, flowing through the hollowgrass's stem. "She set up a transfusion like this one. And when I woke in the morning . . . " He let out a sob. "When I awoke she was dead. She must have passed out . . . There was blood everywhere. She . . . She died . . . to save my wretched life." Alan trembled, crown to toe. Tears burned him more ferociously than the Flame of Ecstasy. A deep coldness had settled into his body, like the icy waters of Hali. He felt dizzy, like he might collapse, and if he did, he hoped the earth would swallow him up, the black mud take him back, like it had the bones of so many monsters.

"Alan . . . " Petruccio said, softly. "Alan?"

"Yes?"

"That's enough. He's waking."

To Alan's surprise, LeBarron's eyes had regained their focus. Gingerly, he lifted his head from the ground, staring up at Alan with idiotic wonder. His features, so elastic, sagged like a septuagenarian's. Alan wondered if this was their natural condition or simply a result of his ordeal. LeBarron swallowed, opened his mouth to speak, then seemed to think better of it. A little colour had returned to his cheeks, but he was still paler than cloud and seemingly just as fragile; he gave a grateful nod.

Petruccio withdrew the hollowgrass stem from LeBarron's arm. Alan removed his own and threw it upon the ground. A single line of blood ran down from the pinprick in his forearm to his stump, where it kissed the Yellow Sign.

"Rose was the reason," Alan said, quietly.

"For what?" Cassilda asked. The shining lamps of her eyes illuminated his spirit.

"The reason my wife left me."

CHAPTER 12:
THE TEMPLE

THERE WAS AN argument about their next course of action. Cali wished to press on, a fact which shocked Alan, though he was beginning to realise Cali's feelings about LeBarron were purely carnal and did not extend to the realm of deep emotion. LeBarron himself was too out of it—drifting in and out of consciousness—to object or suffer hurt feelings.

Despite her concern for time wasted, and her dislike of The Stranger and all his servants, Cassilda was the one to advocate that they spend at least a day resting. If they forced LeBarron to trek now, all the work they had done to save him would be in vain. Alan was also weakened from the transfusion.

Petruccio felt there was danger in both choices. When the patrol failed to return, it was likely another larger one would be sent to investigate what had happened. They would be overwhelmed by more soldiers.

Unable to reach consensus, the deciding vote fell to Alan.

He paced back and forth, weighing up the options. LeBarron had taken a serious wound. Even with the transfusion and stitches, Alan wondered whether he would make it. There was no telling what kind of internal damage had been done. As far as he could tell, the sword had not penetrated as deeply as it could have, but the original stab had been in the approximate area of the kidneys, which was almost always fatal. LeBarron needed a modern hospital. Surgery. Not back-alley stitches.

"A-Alan . . . "

He turned and saw LeBarron staring at him. His eyes were droopy. Consciousness seemed a near-fatal effort. Yet, his gaze was surprisingly steady.

Alan crouched beside LeBarron.

"I'm here, friend."

LeBarron smiled dreamily.

"I have to tell you . . . "

"What?"

"The Stranger, He knows you."

Alan felt his blood run cold.

"How does he know me? What do you mean?"

"I spoke with Him . . . " LeBarron whispered. He swallowed down a bolus of spit, and his entire body shuddered with the effort. " . . . on the other side. I went to that place, Alan. Where everyone takes off their mask . . . "

Perhaps he was delusional—blood loss could cause the same hallucinations as oxygen deprivation because the circulatory system was no longer feeding the brain. Yet, Alan *wanted* to believe his words.

"What is this place?"

LeBarron smiled.

"We think we're the actors, Alan. But we're not. We're only the costumes He puts on, the masks He wears. That is the secret of the Pallid Mask. *We're* the mask, Alan. *We* are." LeBarron had grown passionate, his eyes foaming stars in the deathly brilliance of his face. Whereas before he'd lain almost paralytic, now he rose up on one elbow, gripping Alan's robes with the other in a tight fist. "But He knows you. He told me your name before I ever met you. He said you were coming to save Carcosa . . . " Suddenly LeBarron let go of Alan and fell to the ground. A look of horror contorted his features for a moment, as though Alan had suddenly revealed a plague-pustule, but that horror morphed into wonder. Even in such a condition, LeBarron's performance was enthralling. "Why do you come before me now? Why! The Pallid Mask! I see it! It's you! I cannot bear your light! I cannot bear it!"

"Hush," Alan said, "You are delusional."

He laid a hand on LeBarron and he calmed, suddenly lying very still, although his breathing remained shallow and rapid. It reminded Alan of a dog he'd seen in the road, its spine broken by a passing car, just waiting to die. He had stroked the dog's head, comforted it, and no sooner had that act of tenderness been performed than it passed, instantly. He prayed that LeBarron would not suffer the same fate.

It seemed LeBarron slept for a few moments, awaking with a sharp inhalation.

"Alan," he said, blinking like someone who had known only a prison's darkness for many years.

"I'm here."

"You saved me . . . "

"I did what I could."

LeBarron smiled.

"You are infuriatingly humble." LeBarron glanced around and saw the others, all pretending to be absorbed in minor tasks, but no doubt listening to every word. "Does the party wait for me?"

"You need to recover your strength."

"No," LeBarron said. "We are easy prey out here. And you did good work. I can stand."

"You're sure?"

"Yes."

LeBarron gingerly rolled onto his elbows, a table-top position, then slowly rocked back, sitting straight. He placed one foot flat on the ground, then another, rising slowly, almost like a yogic ritual. Alan fetched him a clean shirt, which he gratefully donned. There was a little weeping from the stitches, but the sutures held for now. LeBarron walked with a limp, clearly suffering a stab of pain through his side with the severed musculature—Alan hoped nothing more significant had been damaged—but after a while his stride smoothed out. Alan realised he was watching LeBarron stepping back into character.

"Fear not," LeBarron said, jovially. "I shall live to fight another day."

"Put him on the quinel," Cali said. "That will mitigate some of the strain."

LeBarron did not protest, which Alan thought was a rare moment of humility from the actor. They removed the saddlebag from the quinel—Alan wore it around his neck—and with Petruccio's help, giving him a leg up, LeBarron clambered atop the beast of burden. It let out a mournful note. LeBarron chuckled, then clutched his ribs.

"Onward," Cali said.

The final stage of their journey was relatively short compared to the vast distance they had covered in the eight days since their departure from Carcosa. Yet, to Alan, he would remember it as perhaps the longest. Bearing the heavy saddlebag, he felt exceedingly vulnerable. Cali remained constantly alert, her deadly instrument in hand, her ceaseless vigilance setting them all on edge. Cassilda walked beside LeBarron and his quinel. She seemed to have softened toward him. Alan had thought her a cold and imperious person when he first met her, but he was discovering she had deep wells of feeling within her, a softness, a tenderness; she reminded him of Rose, in that regard, though the two women looked nothing alike.

The guilt Alan felt, remembering Rose, was manifold. Of course, his primary guilt was her death, but beyond that there were other, subtler poisons that still coursed through his veins. He felt guilty that he had not only betrayed his wife on a sexual and physical level, but an emotional one too—he had cared more deeply for Rose, and shared more with her, than he ever had done with Sharon. In fact, he hardly thought of Sharon, even now. He realised that she had merely been a smokescreen for him to hide his proclivities from society, to play the game of being a "normal citizen". He felt guilty for having used her this way. *You've used women throughout your whole life,* his inner critic reminded him. *In fact, you use most people. You have this way of convincing them you're the submissive one, when in fact you've got your tentacles into their minds. Look at this lot. You've already got them on your leash . . .*

"You're talkative today," Alan muttered.

Petruccio looked behind him and frowned curiously at Alan. Alan gave no response, wrapped up in his thoughts.

The minutes ticked by like hours. Strange shapes appeared behind veils of mist then melted away. They feared attack every moment, which made each second painful.

Bearing his heavy burden, and trudging through the godforsaken marsh, Alan could not help but think of the sufferers in Dante's hell: traitors who wore mantles of lead, treading on the faces of other damned souls. He had betrayed his wife, and in some ways betrayed Rose, so the punishment was apt.

"There!" Cassilda said, breathlessly.

Ahead, through the fog emitted from fecund pools, they saw a massive shape. A squat tower of black stone cast its shadow over the wild and unruly landscape, a small outpost of defiant order in a realm of abundant chaos. Alan could have wept to see a manmade structure.

THE CLAW OF CRAVING

"The Temple of Namtar," Cali said. "This is where The Claw was sealed, Alan. We're almost there."

"And the pigment too," Petruccio said, excitedly.

"Yes," Cali replied. "That as well."

As they neared the tower, they saw a black entryway. Though it was hard to penetrate the gloom lying beyond it, Alan discerned a spiral staircase descending into the bowels of the earth. His mouth became dry. He had experienced many modern dungeons in his quest for Carcosa, but cave systems and deep undergrounds panicked him. He could feel the weight above him, tonnes and tonnes of rock, and it impressed strange nightmares upon his mind.

"We should tie the quinels to this tree," Petruccio said. Then added: "And hope nothing eats them."

LeBarron dismounted, again with Petruccio's help. The quinels were tied to the tree. Alan and Petruccio took the saddlebags with all their supplies and food which were buried a short distance away under another tree. Petruccio used his axe to carve an X into the trunk, so they would not forget which tree marked their belongings.

"Thou look'st green, Alan," Cassilda remarked. Did he detect a note of humour in her voice? If so, it was the first time he had heard anything like that from her, and it was so subtle that he thought he might be imagining it.

"I will be fine. I don't like going underground much."

Cassilda smiled.

"Thou art a curious example of thy gender, Alan."

He frowned.

"How so?"

"Most men I have known would rather cast themselves into an abyss than admit to fear—a perplexing irony. Yet twice now thou hast admitted thy terror. And more, thou hast revealed thy inner traumas before strangers."

"Before *The* Stranger!" LeBarron piped up.

"Truly thou must be feeling better, rogue," Cassilda said, again with that wafer-thin gold-vein of humour running through her voice.

LeBarron chuckled and continued to ready himself for their descent.

Cassilda turned again to Alan.

"Thou must have had a strong mother."

Alan looked surprised at this.

"I had not thought of it. I suppose . . . she was strong. She ran her own business. She provided for us as much as my father did. But . . . " Alan swallowed.

"What is it?"

"I never felt I knew her. Not really. And I'm not sure she knew me, either."

Cassilda's smile became as mysterious as the oceans of the moon.

"God exists in every man and woman, Alan. And God is infinite and unknowable. Therefore, every person is infinite and unknowable, including thyself, and including thy mother. We may only come to know one another by knowing ourselves. Therefore, thou could'st not know her, for thou did not know thyself."

A shiver passed through Alan at her words. How did she come by such wisdom? He had heard similar ideas expressed by various occult teachers over the years, but never quite so succinctly, and never with such a personal dimension that spoke to him.

He was curious, too, what she meant by God. It was clear her views differed greatly to Cali's.

"I think I would like—" But Alan was cut off as Cali arrived.

"Are we ready?"

Cassilda nodded. Alan followed suit.

Cali smiled.

"Then let us enter."

CHAPTER 13:
THE DESCENT

THE STAIRWELL SPIRALLED downward like a coiling serpent descending a tree-trunk. Only ten or so steps down, it became too dark to see. Cassilda made a noise—perhaps the single hummed note of a song—and suddenly they were surrounded by a soft luminosity. Alan turned to find the source of the light and found Cassilda's flesh aglow. My God, she was an angel! A being of pure light!

"I would not advise staring too long," she said. "Thou might'st burn out thy eyes."

It was true his eyes were already aching, so he averted his gaze back down the stairwell. The image of her, flesh alight as though illuminated from within, stayed with him even in the darkness.

They continued. Cali led the way, followed by Alan, then Petruccio and LeBarron, and finally with Cassilda at the rear.

Alan had been turning over Cassilda's reflections on God. Whereas Cali had proposed a view of the world as a mechanism in which they were the key players or agents, Cassilda's view seemed far more spiritual, almost Quaker-esque. Now, however, he had a new question to turn over in his mind: why was Cali's magic so different from Cassilda's? All of Cali's supernatural feats were performed with her strange instrument, which even now hung across her back as she slowly paced down the spiral staircase. Cassilda, however, had produced the light without an instrument. Unless, of course, her *voice* was the instrument . . . That would be a potent power indeed. And perhaps Cali envied that innate power.

The descent was ominously long and dizzying. The spiral tightly wound around a central stone column, and Alan felt himself leaning dangerously far forwards at times, his internal sense of balance shot away by repetition. He would always catch himself however, putting his good hand on the wall to ground himself.

At last, they reached the bottom, their feet splashing in a few inches of lukewarm water.

"The marshes must be leaking through," Cali said. "This temple has been abandoned for a long time."

Alan thought that it looked very little like a temple at all, and this opinion was further validated when they went through a plain doorway and stepped into a high-walled corridor that ended in a T-junction.

"This isn't a temple," he said, with horror. "It's a maze."

The others stepped out into the corridor with them, Cassilda's light washing the walls with opalescence. The stonework looked as though it sweated oil. The floor was a treacherous pool. If there were holes or other dangerous hazards underneath the surface of the water, it would be nigh on impossible to spot them before they became a problem. Alan tried to banish the thought of small, aquatic nightmares swimming through the ankle-deep flooding . . .

"Yes," Cali said, in answer to Alan's question. "The Temple of Namtar was built to keep out those who would misuse The Claw's power. But luckily for you, myself and Cassilda were taught the secret way through by our father, should the need ever arise."

"It makes sense that Uboth would have hidden the pigment here, as well," Petruccio rambled.

Cali nodded, though Alan felt like she was merely humouring him. Petruccio himself had admitted she was not a believer.

"What if you've forgotten the way?" Alan said, hating how pathetic he sounded, but unable to repress the anxious question.

Cali looked at him sourly.

"I do not forget."

"Well, I agree with Alan," LeBarron said. "I'd like this to be over sooner than later."

Alan nodded at LeBarron, grateful for the support.

Cali smirked and turned.

"It's this way. Keep close, lest you become lost."

At first, it seemed they would navigate the labyrinth's runnels exceedingly quickly. Cali took turns confidently, one after another, barely pausing. The group stayed in close proximity, with Cassilda's light always shining from behind them, illuminating the way forward. It was impossible for anyone to lag behind with the light-source keeping the rear.

But as they went deeper, Alan noticed the water levels creeping slowly higher. At first, it did little to impede their progress other than plant a seed of foreboding in their hearts, but after a while the water reached knee height, and they were having to wade and slosh through the mire. Petruccio suffered even worse, as the water reached his waist. Alan also began to notice markings on the walls. In places, the stone had crumbled. Diagonal gashes scarred the brickwork. And worse perhaps than all of these was a jaundiced discolouration that rose to about eye-level. Alan realised this was an old water-line.

The levels could change—and rapidly.

"If you hear the sound of rushing water . . . " Alan said, trailing off.

"We're dead," Petruccio said. "So don't think about it."

"Ever the pragmatist," Alan replied, and he meant it as sincere praise.

"We're almost there," Cali called back to them. Then she halted, as though she had encountered an invisible barrier. Cassilda's pale light—which had the quality of ethereal moonlight—made Cali's coal-black skin seem like a bottomless ocean.

"What's the matter?" Alan asked.

Cali pointed.

Alan saw that there were three roads ahead. Cali indicated the left-hand way. What looked like a great pile of faeces blocked the path. Black water gushed in from a rend in the ceiling, making no sound. It took Alan a while to comprehend that the faeces were actually stones that had been worn smooth by the continual flow of water. Hence also its silence. Ripples spread out from where the marsh-water above finally joined the underground hallways.

"I had not counted on the place falling apart," Cali muttered, a self-rebuke as much as a confession. She paced the rubble. "I could move the stones, but who knows what kind of cave-in that might cause . . . "

"We can find another way, sister," Cassilda supplied.

Cali snorted.

"This is a maze. There's only one way through."

"Perhaps if this part of the labyrinth has collapsed, another might also be damaged, allowing us an unconventional passage?" Petruccio said.

Alan could have kissed the dwarf. He did not know how likely the theory was to hold up under trial, but any hope was better than none.

"It's possible," Cali said. "I suppose we have no choice."

"I hate to play the Devil's advocate, but we do have another choice . . . " LeBarron said. "Why not turn back? If we die here, buried under stone—or drowned in marsh-water—we will be no good to your mother or Carcosa. It is possible there is a new opening, but equally possible there is *no* opening. If The Claw is beyond reach, we risk our lives needlessly. Perhaps the great King In Yellow shall not miss a measly actor and his friends—" He looked at Alan and Petruccio when he said this. Alan felt a surge of affection for the man that took him a little by surprise. "—but he will certainly miss his two beloved daughters."

"The Stranger speaks sense, perhaps," Cassilda said, "Though I am loathe to admit it. What good will our deaths serve? We can find another way to defeat Pe'kar without The Claw. Our mission to save Mother will be one of secrecy and guile after all. A weapon, perhaps, is of less use than stealth."

Cali's eyes glinted in the semi-darkness.

"I thought better of all of you," she said. "Have you been so cowed by your injury, LeBarron? And you, Alan, did you not promise to help me in exchange for granting you entry into Carcosa? Does the Yellow Sign emblazoned on your very flesh mean nothing?" Her eyes went to each of them in turn. "And sister, you know full well Pe'Kar's power is greater than ours. Even should we sneak into his kingdom, even should we get past all his guards and minions without being seen—a rare feat!—the bonds of our mother's cage will no doubt require powers beyond our magical talents to break. Abandon The Claw and you abandon your own mother to torture and death."

Cassilda's face showed a wounded pride.

"Very well, *sister*." A tightness had returned to her voice. "It's clear thou know'st best. Lead on."

Satisfied, Cali turned her back upon them and took the middle road.

Now a new fear gripped Alan and the others. Whereas before Cali's confident strides had engendered calm in all of them despite their dreadful surroundings, now she faltered at each turning, indecision mounting. The water levels were beginning to rise again, and Alan could hear a hissing sound far off, as though there were even larger breaches in the structural integrity of the temple. At last, Petruccio called out to the party.

"Wait, wait!"

They all halted.

The water was nearly to his chin.

"I cannot go on in this," he said. "I am practically swimming."

"I can carry you," LeBarron said.

"No," Alan interjected. "That would risk tearing the stitches. I'll do it."

Petruccio sighed.

"I know it's undignified," Alan said. "But better than drowning."

Petruccio smiled at Alan's appeal to his practical nature.

"Yes. Better than drowning."

Alan lifted Petruccio up—and for a moment feared he would not be able to complete the action, for the dwarf was a great deal heavier than Alan had anticipated—and managed to situate him on his shoulders. Petruccio's short legs hooked his collarbones, his heels digging into Alan's chest.

"My thanks, Alan."

"It's my—"

A shriek ended their pleasantries. The sound travelled down the lost hallways with the same fury as an oncoming train. For a moment, Alan expected to see headlights speeding towards him, to wake up from a black nightmare—but the only light was Cassilda's soft glow. The shriek echoed three times and then all was silent again.

"Something has taken up residence here," LeBarron said, hoarsely.

"I know that sound," Petruccio whispered.

All eyes turned to him.

"A Eurypterid."

LeBarron laughed, though it was not one of his finest performances, his fear shining through the mask of hilarity.

"They are extinct, my friend."

"We *thought* they were extinct. But perhaps one survived, hiding down here . . . ."

Cassilda and Cali locked eyes. An exchange seemed to be passing between them, though no words were spoken openly. At last, Cali broke the spell.

"It is not Namtar," she said, as though concluding a long discussion. "He may not leave the central chamber until released. And that sounded quite unlike the war-cry of a demon."

"Demon?" Alan said. It was an unwelcome surprise to discover The Claw was guarded, though he supposed he should have guessed. "How many secrets are you keeping, Cali? You have much to explain."

Cali grew wroth at his boldness, then seemed to reconsider.

"It is no secret, only an accidental omission. The others are aware of what guards The Claw. I had forgotten how new you are to this world . . . " Cali's smile became a jester's mockery. " . . . you fit in so well with its madness."

"Whatever the case, it appears The Claw has a new guardian," Petruccio said. "We must hurry."

Now attempting jogging pace, they waded through the water. The shriek sounded again, and they all froze.

"The water . . . " Petruccio said. "It can feel the vibrations in the water."

"It's *not* a Eurypterid," LeBarron said.

"What is that?" Alan asked, desperately.

"Something thou dost not wish to meet," Cassilda said. "I shall dim my light."

"No!" Petruccio hissed. "Then we shall risk plummeting into some unseen abyss!"

"I can see without the light," Cali argued. "Dim, sister."

Cassilda seemed to inhale, sucking in a breath—a sound like a falling note, or a sighing lover—and the light faded from moonlight to the even more distant illumination of stars.

"Each of us put a hand on the shoulder of the one before," LeBarron said.

Alan put his good hand on Cali's pauldron. LeBarron on Petruccio—who was still sat on Alan's shoulders. And lastly Cassilda touched LeBarron. They went forward in this centipede configuration. Alan could not help but think of the arthropleura, and wondered if Petruccio were mistaken, and it was merely another one of those creatures haunting the labyrinth. Somehow, he doubted it. The shriek had sounded like nothing he'd encountered before, in this world or the one he had left behind. And Petruccio's knowledge of wildlife seemed impeccable.

They moved more slowly, trying not to disturb the waters. Each felt as though something terrible formed in the shadows around them, every horridly angulated corridor a potential hiding spot for a predator of nightmare; but worse, the waters now rising to the solar plexus offered infinite possibilities for concealment: whatever was coming could rise up underneath them, unseen and unstoppable.

"Hurry, hurry!" Cassilda breathed.

Alan hated how noisome their progress was, each step creating a loud *slosh* that sent ripples through the water. It would have been easy enough for a human being to track them, let alone some creature attuned to the dark and water.

"We should be coming around to the back of Namtar's chamber," Cali said. "Yes. See, this wall, the stones are different."

Alan could see no difference, but held his tongue. Now was not the time for pessimism.

The shriek sounded again, closer this time.

"Look for an opening of any kind!" Cali commanded.

The group scattered and though the corridor was long, there were no turns, so they could keep each other in sight—as far as Cassilda's illumination extended. Alan ran his hands over the brickwork but could find no join unplugged by mortar. LeBarron took a deep breath and then plunged beneath the waters, looking for openings hidden under the surface. He emerged moments later drenched but disappointed.

"We'll never find one," Petruccio said. "You must blast a hole in the wall, Cali."

Cali showed teeth.

"That could collapse the labyrinth."

"At least, then, it shall kill the eurypterid!"

"It cannot be—" But LeBarron protestations were cut short as he seemed to feel, preternaturally, a disturbance. He threw himself forward, like a diver, and just where he had been moments before something colossal erupted from the inky waters. In the half-light of Cassilda's magical illumination, Alan did not comprehend its full horror. He saw merely a flash of gleaming plates, claws, seaweed-like fronds, and a colossal tail, the barbed point of which flashed like a thrown dagger, scoring a deep wound in the wall inches from Alan's head. Petruccio screamed—though it seemed he was unharmed.

LeBarron emerged seconds later frantically kicking as claws tried to snare him. Alan was seized by a heroism he did not feel, a possession of spirit. He watched himself in stupefied horror as he ran forward and kicked downward into the water, his foot connecting with something horribly bony and wide. LeBarron gasped and slipped away, getting his feet under him. A shadow moved under the water past Alan.

"Run!" Petruccio was screaming. Then the dwarf, frustrated by Alan's paralysis, threw himself backwards off Alan's shoulders, landing in the swelling waters below. He began to kick towards LeBarron and the sisters.

The eurypterid, for surely this had to be the creature Petruccio and even Cassilda were so terrified of, rose slowly from the flooding, scummed and wet, resembling a great cluster of rubble hoisted from a pelagic seabed, inscribed with the death-notes of a civilisation. For the first time, Alan stared into its eyes, which were—for all its monstrosity—its worst and most horrifying feature. They were eyes that knew no intelligence, that had no memory. Black coins side by side, featureless and idiot, far too close together—as if they mocked human features. Alan knew far less about the animal kingdom than Petruccio, but he remembered one little factoid from his explorations into the origins of things: a key to distinguishing predator from prey was in the eyes. Prey often had eyes either side of the head to give them greater lateral vision and to detect hidden approaches. Predators, on the other hand, had their eyes next to each other and both facing forward, so that they could focus on their next meal. If there was ever evidence needed that human beings were the apex predator, it was in the eyes, so close together, facing forward with indomitable fixation on whatever conquest they sought next.

This *thing* shared that human trait. Its eyes were set into flat bone, close together yet so alien as to send a chill of dread from crown through the core of Alan's being.

With a wet sound, an orifice too shapeless and reeking to be considered a mouth peeled open, organs within—for which Alan had no name—producing excited sounds.

He was so transfixed with horror he did not react to its scorpion-like tail rising, poised to impale him. Alan had survived so much, done so much, yet in this moment survival instincts failed him; perhaps the long journey through the marsh and loss of blood had worn him down, or perhaps he had always wanted to die . . .

"Do what thou wilt!" he found himself saying.

The eurypterid surged toward him.

CHAPTER 14:
THE SACRIFICE

"**A**LAN!"
LeBarron's hands closed around Alan's waist, wrenching him backward. They both collapsed, plunging beneath the surface of the marsh-water. A blind panic took Alan as he kicked, unable to draw air into his lungs.

Then time slowed. He remembered the second trial at *The Black Star,* that deep cold in which he had been submerged for . . . Cali wouldn't say how long. *You're alive. Calm yourself. Eternity exists in this moment.*

Alan felt his consciousness retreating: not blacking out, but rather expanding to the point where his sense of individuality was redundant, laughable even. How could the water drown him? He *was* the water. And the stone. And the eurypterid too . . .

Something plunged into the water: the eurypterid's tail descending, striking where Alan had stood moments before, an eruption of muddy liquid splashing the tunnel walls. The eurypterid shrieked in frustration, realising it had missed its prey.

LeBarron hauled Alan to his feet—both gasped as they broke the surface and sucked in lungfuls of air. Personhood—and the accompanying fear of death—returned to Alan and they retreated together, scampering through the high floodwaters.

Cali stepped forward. Her chthonic instrument was in her hands, eerily like a human cadaver robbed of its flesh. Her fingers plucked harsh, strident notes.

But if the eurypterid was affected by her power, it gave no indication. Unlike the Pe'karian soldiers who had foamed and seizured upon hearing her bone-chilling melody, the eurypterid continued to cut through the water, surging toward them with fiendishly single-minded intent.

Cali's eyes widened.

"It . . . it has *no ears* . . . "

The scorpion-creature pounced, massive claws flashing. Cali became a dancer, pirouetting over the creature's razor-sharp limbs and landing on the other side. Alan marvelled. She was stronger than any normal human being—how else could she jump so high from a starting position in such deep water?

But his wonder at her athleticism soon turned to panic. In leaping, Cali had to cast aside her potent instrument. The creature's claws flashed, shattering it into flotsam.

Oh God . . . What would Cali be able to do now?

The eurypterid had now set its dismal eyes on Cassilda. Its colossal tail slammed down into the water, nearly flattening Petruccio, and propelling it forward like a torpedo, screeching as it went.

Cassilda seemed so vulnerable, a single blade of pale grass before a tempest. Yet, she showed white teeth, and raised her hands, the shining aura of her flesh brightening and brightening until all had to turn away. The eurypterid halted, its massy bulk slipping and thrashing in the water, its clawed foremost appendages rising to shield its primeval eyes from the blinding light.

"Burn wretch!" Cassilda screamed.

The creature began to lash and roil in throes of pain, its tail whipping backward and forward. As its tail slammed into the wall that separated them from The Claw's chamber, brick and mortar buckled beneath the force of the blow. A crack appeared, and through it shone a golden light that speared into their hall like a lightning bolt frozen the moment it flashed. This light had a different quality to Cassilda's near-blinding radiance. This was a tarnished brightness, as though after long eons even light could rust.

Dust rained from the ceiling, followed by small stones, and then a gush of black liquid. Cali had been right, the place was just a breath away from crumbling around them.

LeBarron drew his sword and leapt forward, hacking two-handed on the tail of the thrashing eurypterid. His steel bounced off its hardened armour plates, and then it swept its massive limb at LeBarron. He dived beneath the waters. The creature was now trying to turn around, bending like a serpent. It did not want to look at the light. But its massive bulk was making the movement difficult.

Now, Alan thought. *Now while it's stuck we have a chance.*

Petruccio had emerged from the waters, which were dangerously high for him. His small axe glinted in his hand. Limbs that seemed more like fronds of seaweed than legs jittered and wetly slapped against the stone and floor, scrabbling for purchase. Screaming like a wild animal, Petruccio began to hack at them. The creature squealed, still contorted and pinned, and Alan saw its limbs dropping from its torso as Petruccio went to work. The dwarf had a fiercely strong hand. His face, covered in the nameless ichor spraying from the severed appendages of the nightmare creature, had hardened into a resolve like granite. LeBarron joined the dwarf's side, now able to get right under the creature, perhaps the point of greatest danger, but also where its soft underbelly resided.

Its crab-like fore-claws swung down at LeBarron. Unlike Petruccio, he was a much easier target. The actor was lithe, however, dodging the clumsy swings. Then he drove his blade up, to the hilt, into the creature's stomach. The shriek that it emitted from an orifice that had not yet learned to become a mouth would chill Alan for the rest of his life—it would echo in his dreams and awaken him from sleep, where he would sit listening for many hours to the wind, hoping against hope he had mistaken the moans of air for that alien and godless scream.

The pain gave it new strength. Thrashing, it turned fully about and extricated itself from the narrow hold of the corridor. Its stinger-tail whipped past Alan's head, and had Cassilda not ran and dragged him down, he would have been decapitated. Instead, the tail smashed into the wall where it further buckled, more golden light spearing into the hallway through a large crack, the brickwork giving way like jigsaw pieces when a child is finally bored of the complete image and uses their thumbs to leverage the joins apart again.

"You took my instrument from me, beast," Cali snarled. "The labour of centuries, both in body and spirit! For this, your fate shall be truly terrible!"

If the creature understood her—or its peril—it gave no sign. It lurched toward her, claws snapping.

Cali raised a fist and brought it slamming down on the dome-plated head of the creature. If Alan had doubted her powers without the instrument, he needn't have. The force of the blow split super-hardened chitin—harder than steel—as though it were an eggshell. The thing collapsed, twitching into the water. Cali struck again. And again. Its massive body spasmed with each blow. After the fifth strike, peabrain leaked from its fractured skull, and it no longer twitched. Its eyes were just as soulless in death as in life.

Cali let out a sigh of exhaustion, steadying herself on the wall. Her fist was a bloodied mangle. Despite her power, she had hurt herself smashing apart the eurypterid's defences. She cradled the hand. Alan was certain she had broken fingers and the small bones of her palm.

"Well done, all," LeBarron said, jovially. Alan grinned. His smile quickly disappeared, however, when he saw red at LeBarron's side.

"Your sutures are torn," Alan said.

LeBarron grimaced.

"Only a little. I will be fine."

"We should really harvest its armour," Petruccio said. "We'd be rich!"

Alan had found the answer to which creature supplied the curling platemail worn by Carcosa's soldiers: it was eurypterids.

"I cannot believe your people hunt these for their plate."

"Hunt?" Petruccio frowned. "Oh no. Far too dangerous. Those watchmen you saw are kitted out in fossils. That platemail was scavenged from the marshes. A new set like this would hence be worth a small fortune."

"We lack means of transportation," LeBarron said. The plates did look like they weighed a great deal.

"It is not what we came here for . . . " Eyes turned to Cassilda, who had allowed her blinding light to dim again to tolerable levels. Her expression was curious, a mixture of sadness and triumph, the delicate lines of her face bent like bamboo beneath a light wind.

"Thank you for saving me," Alan said.

Cassilda smiled.

"Thou art reckless, Alan Chambers. But I cannot say it is entirely a fault."

Cali did not partake of celebrations. She was already moving to the place where the wall had been weakened by the beast's thrashings. With one cursory glance at the ceiling, which may even have been a prayer, she forced some of the loose bricks out of their moorings, creating a narrow opening that, side-on, a thin person could slip through.

"Come," she said. "We're here."

Alan frowned. When his journey had begun, Cali had seemed so exquisitely in control. He could not have imagined her flustered by anything. Passionate, perhaps, but never perturbed or wrongfooted—certainly in no rush. The closer they had come to The Claw, however, the more strangely she'd seemed to behave, almost like an addict who had been leading them towards an old stash of heroin they'd buried for a rainy day. She now seemed driven by a secret purpose, and the illusion of control she had presented to Alan was melting away. A mania lit Cali's serpentine eyes as she disappeared through the sliver-gap in the wall.

Alan looked at Cassilda, trying to frame his expression into that of a question. But if Cassilda held the answers, she gave no sign, but lowered her eyes to the ground.

"Cali is right," Petruccio said. His voice trembled slightly. Was he thinking about the pigment, in that moment? "We shouldn't linger. We've been given a window—literally. Let's take it."

The dwarf slipped through the gap.

LeBarron bowed and pointed, indicating Alan go first.

"You fought bravely, LeBarron. The honour should be yours."

The actor smiled dazzlingly. Though sweat sheened his face and his skin was an unhealthy colour, greenish and yellow where it should be fleshy, his rugged good looks still held a charm.

"I'm only pretend-brave, Alan. I've told you this."

He squeezed himself through the opening.

Cassilda stood with Alan.

"Thou must go first."

"Why?"

"Because this is thy destiny."

Her smile was at once sweet and terrifying. He wondered how something that seemed so petite, so impossibly delicate and fine, could contain such power. It was like uranium stored inside expensive china.

Alan, coming from a world of modern conveniences, was the largest of the group. By no means fat, but not rake-thin as the rest were. A few more bricks dislodged as he forced himself through the narrow opening. He let out a breath he'd been holding on the other side.

The chamber was square, each wall of equal length. The far wall, opposite to them, had an opening, but it was blocked with piles of rubble and detritus . . .

A sound like a strangled mouse escaped Alan's lips and he stumbled backward. His eyes could not believe what they were seeing.

The eurypterid had been a monster, but in a strange way, its monstrosity was concurrent with his own world. Prehistoric terrors had walked the face of the Earth, and evidence of their former dominance could be found in creatures as common as the household spider, the crocodile, or the shark. The natural world was full of mindless beasts. They made a strange sort of sense.

What now stood before him however plunged far deeper into the uncanny valley of possibilities. Human *and* inhuman at the same time. It had four limbs and a head, like a man. A torso. Fingers. A face . . . But all of these were wrong, profoundly wrong. Its gnarled limbs, too big and gangly for its body, were folded. Its flesh made Cali's seem a brightness. Its eyes were pure-white stars, pupil-less and insane. Even though the chamber rose incredibly high, it seemed the creature could barely fit within it, hunched over, like a child squatting amidst ruins. Its height was difficult to estimate, given its posture, but at full stretch it must have stood twenty feet tall. Black wings sprouted from its back. Its head grew into a colossal cone-like crest that stretched back into darkness and became one with it. For all its hideousness, however, there *was* something beautiful in its strange form.

"Dove-like sat'st brooding on the vast Abyss . . . " Alan whispered, recalling the lines of an old poem. "And mad'st it pregnant." Only such a divine yet bizarrely sexual act could have conceived such a being.

Now Alan saw clearly. The Pe'karians were not true demons. They had remade themselves in the *image* of true demons—one of which crouched before them. He shuddered to think what bodily tortures they had endured to approximate this ancient species—and yet still they were not a sliver as terrible as the original.

"You killed my pet," the demon said, disconsolately.

Cali bowed.

"We apologise, Namtar. We have journeyed far to beseech you."

THE CLAW OF CRAVING

The demon scowled.

"You come seeking this?"

The demon lifted one of its mighty hands, a hand that could have wrapped Alan's entire body and perhaps emptied him with a single squeeze like a tube of toothpaste. In its colossal palm shone what seemed a jagged fragment of gold. *The Claw!* Alan's eyes widened in wonder and his heart pounded. It was not merely a weapon, but an infinite jewel. Its beauty was astounding, mesmerising. Parts of it seemed technological, with cogs and wires and great winding mechanisms sheathed in coppers and silvers and golds. Its talon-fingers sizzled with the same tarnished light that had breached their hallway: electricity? lightning trapped in a bottle?

Other parts of The Claw seemed less mechanical and more . . . organic. Panels of leathern skin gave way to gem-studded musculature. Ligaments shone like cables. At the place where it joined the wrist horrid, spiked contraptions extended, the purpose of which Alan could guess at but did not wish to comprehend.

The demon closed his palm, the light dimmed, and he returned The Claw to some unseen hiding place—perhaps within his own being.

Cassilda now joined them in the chamber. Alan noticed her trembling slightly as she beheld the giant demon. Even Cali seemed deferential before it. Could it be the demon was more powerful than them both? If so, what was to stop it killing them all?

"But first," Petruccio said, stepping forward. "I must ask whether you also have the oneiric pigment in your possession?"

The demon snorted. "No pigment here, dwarf. You have been misled."

Petruccio remained standing.

"That cannot be. In the city, they told me . . . "

"The city of Carcosa is far from here, dwarf," the demon growled. "Had I the pigment, and were able to dream new realities, do you think that I would remain here in confinement, bound to the word of a maniac?"

Petruccio bowed and stepped back, disappointment etched on his face.

Namtar's eyes scanned each of them, lingering a disturbing length of time upon Alan, before finally resting on Cali.

"Haercus wagered that he could defeat me without the use of

104

his Claw . . . " the demon said. "To my shame, he won that wager, and so I was sworn to uphold what I vowed: to guard The Claw. Therefore, there are two choices before you. Either you might try to take The Claw from me by force." The demon snorted, and a momentary grin showed teeth like coals. "Or you may pay the common price to dissolve a demon's vow."

Cali nodded.

"We have not come to fight, Namtar. Your might is well known to us. We will pay the price—and in the process, free you from your bondage."

The demon smiled and let out a sigh that blew a fell wind through the chamber, almost unsteadying Alan on his feet. The pleasure in that sigh raised his hackles and sent a chill down his spine.

"Oh, how long I have waited for one to pay my ransom. You shall know the gratitude of one of the great demons, Cali of Carcosa . . . "

Cali smiled.

"Now," the demon said, licking its lips. "Bring the virgin before me."

CHAPTER 15:
THE TRUTH

A DARK SILENCE followed this command. Alan watched each of his companions, struggling to make sense of it. His eyes rested on Petruccio, who had turned white as a sheet, trembling head to toe.

"Cali!" Petruccio hissed. His face was a wounded mask not even LeBarron could have simulated. The venom with which he uttered her name revealed black depths of betrayal.

"I'm sorry, Petruccio. Truly," Cali said, softly. "But virgin blood is the only thing that may break a demon's vow. You should be honoured—your virtue will save Carcosa."

The dwarf shook, with both rage and terror.

"You tricked me! Tricked us all!"

Alan did not know how his brain was able to compute all the variables so rapidly, but with a dream-knowing he realised what was happening: Petruccio was a virgin—hence why he had been able to resist Cali for so long, simply serving her without becoming a deeper slave. Cali had known this from the start, which meant she had also come here *knowing* he would need to be sacrificed to Namtar.

Alan had done bad things in his time: abandoned men and women he should have loved, made selfish decisions, pushed his family away, put the pursuit of his desires above all else, but the cold calculation of Cali's manoeuvre sickened him in a way he had not known he could be sickened.

Petruccio launched himself at the black princess. Cali lifted him by the throat as effortlessly as though he were a mere bundle of clothes and hurled him toward the feet of the demon.

"I weigh your life against the lives of all Carcosa," she said.

106

"Your quest for the oneiric pigment is a madman's errand, Petruccio. Would it not be better to die with purpose than live in vain?"

The dwarf did not move.

"Cali . . . " LeBarron said. "That is . . . cold."

She turned on her lover.

"It doesn't matter what is right in your eyes," Cali said, darkness shining from her flesh. "All that matters is desire, and the will to act upon it. You can't *imagine* the length of time I have waited . . . "

Cassilda sneered. She stepped forward towards Cali, and it seemed to Alan a new energy burned from her, as though her fire had turned sulphuric.

"O sister, thou hast overplayed thy hand. Thou art outnumbered. And now I see the truth of thy soul. How long hast thou loved Pe'kar?"

A terrible silence fell upon the room. Alan's heart dropped through his stomach and onto the floor. The sword of his mind slashed to and fro, trying to cut through the illusion that Cassilda's words had raised before him, but they could not, for it was no illusion. Alan saw it clearly now, how all Cali's actions and motivations revealed a secret purpose. She had slain the Pe'karians so they would not reveal her true nature. She had flirted with Alan in the beginning to win his loyalty. She had resented Cassilda coming on the journey lest she be exposed.

She had played them all for fools, but as Cassilda said, she had gone one step too far in offering up Petruccio, overestimating the power of her personality. *Hubris!* The oldest and deepest sin. Alan smiled darkly, for it was perhaps one of the few sins he did not stand in danger of.

Cassilda seemed to be rising, growing, like a thundercloud reaching maximum potential before unleashing its deadly payload.

"How evil thou art, sister, to use this man so!" She indicated Alan.

"And me!" LeBarron said, never missing an opportunity for theatre, even in the midst of terrible danger.

"Evil?" Cali sneered. "Is it evil to want a future for Carcosa? You live in the past, sister. And you have infected the entire city with your obsession."

Cassilda ignored the insult. "I insisted upon coming with thee because I have long suspected thy motives. Now, all becomes clear. *Traitor!*" Cassilda trembled with rage. "Tell me, was it *you* that ordered Mother's capture?"

Cali smiled a terrible smile, an Emperor Nero grinning at the end of the world.

"It seems subterfuge has failed. But you must know, sister, I suspected you might uncover my true intentions. That is why I *allowed* you to come. Out here, I may dispose of you, and no one in Carcosa will know."

Cassilda glittered with thunderous potential. Tears ran down her cheeks bright as lightning forks.

"Then let us dance, Cali!"

"When I have killed you, *sister* . . . " Cali spat the word. Then her eyes turned on Alan. "I shall make *you* do my bidding. You think I cannot compel you? You know *nothing* of Carcosa!"

Cali had no more time to boast, for Cassilda descended upon her in a flash of lightning.

The rage of those two women blazed like an inferno. A shockwave spread from the point of their contact and Alan, LeBarron, and Petruccio were thrown back.

Namtar the demon watched all: unblinking, bored.

Alan scrabbled to his feet. Cassilda was a streak of white lightning, but Cali became the black storm clouds enveloping her. The next moment Cassilda seemed a white bird, and Cali a wolf, sinking black teeth into her side. Cassilda screamed. In a blink, she was a tremendous albino serpent, curling around and sinking fangs into Cali. As Cali howled, she became a mongoose, then something stranger still. On and on it went, their forms shifting, blurring sense, their anatomies becoming increasingly distorted and terrible; blasts of power shook the room, causing dust to fall from the ceiling. Terrible musical notes resonated. Alan touched his ear and found it bleeding. The notes were the women's voices, trying to unmake one another.

Despite the cacophony, Petruccio lay unconscious by the demon's feet. Namtar looked down at him, a smile spreading across his twisted features.

"No!" LeBarron cried. "No, great demon, you cannot take him! We rescind our offer!"

Namtar scowled. He let out a snort that sent volcanic heat through the air.

LeBarron circled the women, blade in hand, looking for an opening. Alan noticed him clutching his side. Blood dripped through his fingers.

All was coming undone.

"LeBarron!" he cried.

The actor turned woozy eyes on him.

"What do we do?" Alan begged.

"We've been used, Alan. We should take the dwarf and run!"

It made so much sense. What did he owe Cali now? And Cassilda, he barely knew her. Yes, they had been used, so it was only right to abandon them to whatever fate remained.

No.

The voice that had so often chided Alan had returned. Now, in the midst of the thunder around them, it spoke with quiet authority.

You spent your life using women, using men, using everyone. Now you know what that feels like.

Alan gritted his teeth.

"We'll die if we stay."

And she will die if you don't.

Alan saw Cassilda and Cali's fight still unfolding, though now it was becoming clear that Cassilda was losing. She was a lioness, trampled beneath a terrible horned thing; a swan seized in the jaws of a nameless reptile; a glistering fish devoured in the mouth of an ancient shark, the lower lip of which curled back on itself like a bladed tentacle. More and more often, Cali was coming out on top. Alan could hear, amidst the sonic haze, the dissonance of Cassilda's screams. Her face shone through the illusions, bloodied and broken. She could not endure much more. Cali's serpentine eyes glittered from the black clouds, ecstatic with anticipation of victory.

The image resolved, and Cali stood atop Cassilda, pinning her to the floor with a foot Alan once would have paid money to kiss, to feel stamping upon him, to worship. Cassilda's dress, already soiled from their journeys, was now stained red. Her face was pulped and broken. Her hair had been violated with crimson. She turned quivering features on Alan. Only one good eye could look out, blinking. Her lips formed the words *Run*.

Cassilda turned her eyes back on her sister, and let out a roar, guttural and rending. Cali startled backward as a snowy bear erupted from beneath her. A second later, Cali was an elephant seal, tusked and ugly, and the two beasts were striking each other with tectonic force.

Cassilda was buying them time. She was sacrificing herself for them.

But Alan could not run. Not now.

"We have to get The Claw!" Alan said to LeBarron. "It's the only way we can help Cassilda!"

LeBarron looked at him with surprise, then nodded. They both stumbled away from the whirlwind at the heart of the chamber, at once a cyclone, a crystal ball of dream-visions, and nuclear fusion about to detonate.

Alan approached Namtar, barely able to keep his breathing even. The demon towered over him. Over the course of his occult forays, Alan had associated with many who claimed to be able to summon demons, and even to bind them to their will, but seeing this potentate, Alan doubted any of them had seriously succeeded. He could not imagine the power required to enslave a being such as this.

"We need The Claw!" he said.

The demon sneered.

"You know the price, *gimp*."

Alan cast around. "Is a virgin sacrifice truly the *only* way in which you may be released from your bond?"

The demon considered.

"That, or the one who bound me must release me from the debt. But he is long dead."

Alan smiled.

"No, Great Namtar, thou art mistaken." He put on his best theatre voice. "Haercus is here with us now . . . " Alan swept his hands and pointed at—but LeBarron was no longer there. In his place stood a haughty warrior, clad in bestial arms, shoulder-pads made from the beaks of colossal eagles, his hauberk wrought of serpent scales, his eyes painted black as shadow—his right hand ending in a stump, just like Alan's. His every facial feature was hawk-like and pointed, as though each bone in his body strained to become a weapon.

Namtar hissed.

"It has been a long time, Namtar," Haercus rumbled.

"Trickster, deceiver, liar!" Namtar snarled, and for a moment Alan thought the demon might throw aside his vows and attack the vision of his past without a care for the consequences, but he pulled back, straightening. It reminded Alan of a drug addict desperate to remain on the right side of the one who held the keys to their addiction, however much they hated them.

"I had thought you slain three eons ago by Lord Pe'kar?"

"Nay," Haercus said. "Rumours spread by my enemies. He did leave me a scar, however." Haercus lifted a fold of his armour, and showed the ghastly wound in his side. Reality and illusion dangerously overlapped and Alan felt dizzy.

The demon chortled.

"I wish to return the favour," Haercus said. "I need my Claw back, and thus, I plan to release you."

Namtar's eyes widened. But just when Alan thought they had made it, and Namtar would hand over The Claw without another word, the star-bright orbs narrowed into glowing slits.

"If this is some trick . . . "

"No trick, Namtar. You have suffered for our wager. And I now need The Claw again."

"But what of these . . . others?" Suspicion weighted the demon's words. "Why have they come?"

"They came to bear witness," Haercus said. "But they have gone mad at the sight of The Claw. You should not have shown it to them, Namtar. You know how such power drives mortals mad."

"Except you," the demon hissed.

"I am already mad," Haercus replied.

A snarl that seemed also a grimace of respect made the demon's features into a patchwork madness, but then they settled, and Namtar lifted his huge hand, opening his fingers, revealing the golden Claw.

"I release you, Namtar!" Haercus whispered.

Namtar trembled, his every limb vibrating.

"Ten eons and at last, at last, I am released! *Free!*" Then he rose, not just standing on his feet, but beating his wings. Like a luminous vampire bat he hurled upwards into the vaults of the chamber and with a thunderous crash smashed through the stone and gained open air. The demon's defiant roar was of thunder hurled back at its creator.

Black marsh-water descended on them from the opening. In the demon's wake lay the golden talisman. As the water rose it still glittered beneath the surface. Alan scrambled forward, sweeping his good hand through the waters, finally catching hold of a bladed talon. Instantly, it cut his palm. Wincing, he dragged it from the muck.

"Alan . . . "

He turned. LeBarron stood before him again, or rather leaned against one wall, clutching his side, which was leaking disgusting volumes of blood. LeBarron gulped, struggling for air. He had given all to ensure his performance was watertight.

"LeBarron, you're hurt . . . "

"I will be fine. Acting is . . . tiring work."

"Thank you . . . for everything."

The actor slumped down against the wall.

"Go save the princess . . . " The actor grinned. "Now there's a line from a play!"

His head lolled to one side, and he lay very still. Alan could not tell if he was dead or unconscious. Alan quickly dragged Petruccio's limp body upright and lay him next to the actor, ensuring neither drowned in the water pouring down into their chamber.

At last, he turned to face the two sisters. Their fight had slowed, their transformations coming less rapidly, but their blows landing harder. Cassilda now lay in her true form on the floor, blood spilling from her mouth. Cali stood over her, gripping her by the throat, bringing her already broken fist down like a sledgehammer with punitive force against her sister's face. Those features Alan had so admired were broken and smashed. Purple blotches and lumps made Cassilda's visage into a bubonic disaster-piece. Blood leaked from one eye. Her nose was a smear across one cheek. She was missing teeth.

Cali, though bearing some wounds, by contrast looked relatively unharmed.

"You always acted like you were better than me," Cali sneered. "But you are *so weak*."

"At least I'm not a puppet," Cassilda spat.

"Puppet? You think I serve Pe'kar? No. Pe'kar is a tool, sister, to deliver me what I truly want. *I* am going to become the new King In Yellow."

"The demon lord has poured poison in thy ear," Cassilda snarled. "Thou art not thyself, and thou knowest it."

"Spare me your revolting pretensions," Cali said. "You could at least die with some degree of honesty."

Cassilda smirked.

"Fuck you, then."

Cali grinned.

"That's more like it."

Cali raised her hand to deliver the killing blow.

"Let her go!" Alan said.

CHAPTER 16:
THE CLAW

THE SENSATION OF The Claw bonding to Alan's flesh could not be described. Metal impregnated his wrist—right where the Yellow Sign lay—and he screamed as he felt artificial ligaments boring down through the musculature of his forearm. He gripped his wrist with his left hand, now wishing to undo what he had done, but there was no turning back. Electrical currents surged down his arm, then through his whole body. His teeth fizzled. His eyes glowed phosphorously bright. He felt the coils of organic wires ensnaring his nerve-endings. Felt a burn as though a blacksmith had taken a blowtorch to his ligaments, soldering them to The Claw's mechanisms. Where metal and flesh touched all was burning agony.

Now, thou art whole, Alan Chambers.

The voice sounded through Alan's screams. It was the same arch, critical voice that had haunted him throughout his entire voyage. He had thought it was an aspect of himself, the "voice inside his head" that so many neurotics and self-critics described, but no, it was something more than that, something *outside* of himself. The voice had grown stronger once he entered the lands of Carcosa, and now he realised it *was* Carcosa.

"Who are you?" Alan choked.

I am that which lies dreaming within you.

As suddenly as the sensations had arisen, the pain ended. Alan sat on his knees, still clutching his wrist with his left hand. Smoke and the smell of charred flesh rose from his new appendage, cruelly gleaming like Freddy Kruger's vicious talons. Even fogged with his excruciations, Alan could not help but marvel at The Claw: its design was haunting, maleficent, insane. He tried to follow the

114

wires and cogs, to understand how the mechanism fitted together, but it had been made by a labyrinthine mind, a mind of mirrors and dark reflections. The talon-fingers made humming noises as they moved through the air. No, as *Alan* moved them through the air. Each finger responded as though it were a part of him.

Alan wondered what kind of effort of will Haercus had exerted to remove such an implement. Not only was The Claw bonded deeply, a part of his flesh, but Alan had no desire to relinquish it. For the first time in his life, he felt power surging through his veins. Lightning crackled, playing between the bladed talon-fingers. Alan flexed the hand, opening it wide and then closing it so that the horrid claws thunked against his metal palm.

At last, he looked up, locking eyes with Cali.

"Well, my sweet," she said. "You have come quite far indeed. Did I not tell you all answers lie in Carcosa? That you would find much to replace what was lost?"

Alan rose on trembling legs.

"Let her go, Cali."

"My sister?" Cali sneered. "No, Alan. I can appreciate that I have been painted as a villain, but you must understand, I truly do wish to save Carcosa. To save it from itself. The city is rotting—you saw as much with your own eyes. It's time for a new leader. But in order for the city to be reborn, old ways must die." She smiled. "You know of what I speak. You burned in the Flames of Ecstasy. You felt the death of your ego, the transcendence into something greater! The old must be burned away so that the new can live again. This is something your world understands a little better than Carcosa. In a place where lives are eternal, where nothing dies unless it is by wilful act, how can change happen? It cannot. So, I must become the villain. I must become Death. But it is to *save* Carcosa." She extended a hand. "Come with me, Alan. I always wanted you to be my champion. Now, you have The Claw. You succeeded where so many failed. I knew you were special. We can rule together. I can be your queen." Her voice had lowered into a deeper register, a purring seduction. Her unblinking eyes bored into his. She resembled the serpent, but in truth she was the snake charmer. "Us. Together. Forever. Imagine what we could do . . . "

A dark temptation came upon Alan. He felt its presence like a physical entity, a lustrous spirit, swaddled in black robes, cooing into his ear. He saw himself as Lord of Carcosa, saw Cali at his side, saw her and he locked in a desirous embrace, saw all his secret and dark fantasies fulfilled . . .

And then he saw Daisy. He saw Rose. He saw Cassilda, lying at Cali's feet, a bloodied ruin. Petruccio and LeBarron, both half dead. His heart hardened, and with an expulsion of air the spirit of temptation blew away, no more substantial than dust. Alan raised The Claw, and its esoteric light framed his face in a yellow halo.

"No, Cali. You are treacherous in your every word. You have no desire for me. I saw you and him . . . " He pointed at LeBarron. "You have used me—used all of us—from the beginning."

Cali's lips quirked into a curious expression, both smile and grimace, as though two halves of her self competed for control.

"Then you saw me lie with a *real* man."

Alan laughed.

"You think I have not endured far worse barbs?"

Cali rolled her eyes.

"Forever casting yourself in the role of tragic hero! Forever casting yourself as the victim! How pathetic you are! If you could see anything of the truth you would know there is *nothing* special about you. A million men and women have lived your life, believing wholeheartedly they were some kind of chosen outcast, that one day Carcosa would embrace them. As I told you, outcasts make up the majority of Carcosa's population. You are one of millions, perhaps even billions, sharing the same moronic fantasy of specialness." As she spoke, she seemed to rise in stature, her shadow-kissed body expanding, bleeding shadows from it that writhed upon the ground. "But I, on the other hand, *am* special, Alan. Born of a forbidden union. The blood of gods and demons runs through my veins. What hope do you think you have against me? I will crush you like the bug you are and take The Claw."

"No," Alan whispered.

Her smile became feral.

"You think you'll stop *me*? *You?*" Laughter rang around the chamber. "I can smell your fear!"

"I am afraid," Alan whispered. "I am afraid that the chrysalis has finally been shed. I am afraid that the secret flower of the Self is finally in bloom . . . " His eyes were lit with mania. Slowly, he began to raise The Claw; an awful yellow light spilled from it, like a cup overflowing with venomous potential. Cali's shadow was forced backward by the potency of that xanthous shine. Crackling power coruscated around his bladed fingertips. Alan's robes fluttered in a wind of black lightning. "I am afraid, Cali, but not of *you*. It is my *own* true face I fear!"

Cali blanched, then recoiled backward as though burned. Alan thrust his hand into the air, and now spewing from The Claw were violent yellow serpents. They slithered along the ground, the crepitation of thunder accompanying their movements.

She seemed to rally her courage, throwing up her hands, creating a black wall that momentarily repelled the serpents. Still more power burst from The Claw, erupting as though from the peak of a volcano. Alan's eyes were only yellow light. His entire body trembled as though it were the very fulcrum of a rotating solar system, every gravity acting upon it at once. The chamber was filled with awful colours. Shadows died beneath the spearing light of a diseased star.

"You are mine, Alan Chambers!" she roared.

"You can have him," the Claw-wielder said. "I cast off that name."

Cali's eyes widened.

"No!" she hissed.

"Yes," the Claw-wielder cried, his smile a dazzle of sunflowers. A rumbling sounded as of a cloud of wasps. Locusts swarmed down from the aperture in the ceiling and formed a cyclone about him. All that was yellow belonged to him, was a part of him, and still the currents of lighting thickened, intensified, sparked and lashed. Cali could barely hold them back. "I have discovered my secret Self. And when I learn my true name, no god or demon will stand against me."

Cali gritted teeth.

"Then I kill you now."

"I think not, Cali. I am The Claw that grasps reality. And I choose *life!*"

When the man who had once been Alan Chambers spoke that word, the force that erupted from The Claw was obliterating. One moment, Cali stood before him, an equal. The next, she had been thrown through solid stone, burned as if imprisoned upon the surface of the sun, and scoured by tongues of lightning that hungered for her flesh like starved serpents. Her scream broke sound itself, then faded as she was buried beneath tonnes of rubble. Structures that had held up the marshes for eons now collapsed and deluges broke into the labyrinth, washing the hallways, and flooding their chamber with a rising water level. Masonry hailed from the ceiling. The entire temple complex was coming apart.

The locusts scattered, swarming up towards open air again. The spell was broken.

Alan—for the light had now faded from his eyes, and a sense of normalcy returned—knew that Cali wasn't dead, but if he went after her into the collapsing tunnels he and the others would surely perish.

"A-Alan."

He ran to Cassilda's side.

"I am here."

She could barely look at him, her face was so swollen. She had suffered these injuries for him and the others. *No, not just for your lives, but for a greater purpose. She believes in something beyond herself. She believes in Carcosa.* Against all the odds, she was smiling.

"You . . . you beat her . . . You really are . . . special." Her formal dialect had vanished, perhaps broken by Cali, and now she addressed him as a woman, as a kindred soul. He was almost moved to tears.

"I have to get you out of here."

She smiled sadly.

"It's alright, Alan. Even princesses die. You did what you could. Cali will have fled. You must warn the city. You *must* stop her . . . "

Alan shook his head.

"No! I'm going to save you all."

Cassilda's eyes turned up to the opening in the ceiling. Black mud and filth rained around them. A piece of stonework detached and fell, splashing only a few feet away. It could easily have crushed them into paste. A dream of sky hovered beyond the scum.

"If I had magic left in me . . . " She coughed and blood ran from her mouth. "But I can't."

Alan looked up again. The opening . . . *up* was the only way out.

"Music . . . magic is music, right?" he said.

Cassilda frowned.

Alan closed his eyes.

He had never been much of a singer. His voice was harsh, and ugly. But The Claw had wrought changes in him beyond merely the physical. It had activated some long dormant current within himself—a filigree of gold buried in excrement, a single harmonious tune amidst a hideous cacophony. He closed his eyes in order to find that tune, to listen to the beauty that was just beginning its overture within.

"Along the shore the cloud waves break," he murmured. "The twin suns sink beneath the lake. The shadows lengthen—in Carcosa."

He opened his eyes and saw Cassilda staring at him with frightening intensity.

"Strange is the night where black stars *rise*," he sang. And now he felt a lightness in his body, as though the sin of his flesh were being shrived, burned away. "And strange moons circle through the skies. But stranger still is . . . "

"Lost Carcosa . . . " Cassilda breathed. Her voice was battered and broken, but still sweeter than Alan's, and as her voice joined his, all four of them—LeBarron and Petruccio still unconscious—began to float. At first, Alan thought that the waters lifted them with buoyancy, but soon they left the waters behind. They were flying!

Light shone from Cassilda's face. Her smile—though missing teeth—was a glory to behold.

"Song that the Hyades shall sing," they sang together. "Where flap the tatters of the King, must die unheard—in Dim Carcosa!"

Now ten feet high, levitating, ensconced in bright light. Now fifteen. Now twenty. Below them the churning cauldron of the foaming marsh-waters seemed to rage at its prey's escape. Alan now turned his eyes upward, to the black and beautiful night sky that greeted them with winking stars.

"Song of my soul!" he cried. "My voice is dead! Die thou unsung, as tears unshed shall dry and die—in Lost Carcosa!"

As effortlessly as though the Hand of God lifted them, the four rose beyond the lip of the broken ceiling, sailed across the ruptured plains, and floated towards the black tower that had marked the entrance to the temple. As the last note of the song trailed off the power that had sustained their flight departed, and they tumbled to the ground. For a moment, all lay there in stillness and silence.

Then, Cassilda started to laugh. Sweeter than music to Alan's ears.

CHAPTER 17:
THE PLAN

ALAN CHECKED THE area and found the quinels gone. Cali must have taken them, as there did not seem to be signs of a struggle. However, he checked where Petruccio had buried the saddlebags and found, to his surprise, Cali had been sloppy, forgetting to retrieve the supplies. Or perhaps, Alan considered, she did not need them. Either way, it was a boon. Otherwise they would have been stranded in the marsh with no food, other than what they could scavenge and hunt.

When he returned to the others, both LeBarron and Petruccio were awake. The dwarf's head hung in deep depression. LeBarron rested against a tree, clutching his side. He looked bleary-eyed, pained, but he smiled as Alan approached.

"I hear that we are once again in your debt, Alan Chambers."

The name still rankled him as odd. It was not his name, anymore, it belonged to another man. But until he found his true name, he would have to make do. He knew, now, that Carcosa would provide him with the answers, just as Cali had promised.

"You owe me nothing. In fact, I owe you. Without your skills, we would never have obtained The Claw."

"We?" LeBarron said, raising an eyebrow. "The Claw only has one master, Alan. And that is you."

"Perhaps. But I intend to use it in service to the greater good."

"Then you are a better man than I," LeBarron said, closing his eyes.

"Petruccio . . . " Alan said, softly.

The dwarf raised his head, met Alan's gaze. There was a red welt across his neck, a permanent mark, perhaps, from Cali's hand.

"I feel the cosmic fool."

"She deceived us all. Even her own sister."

Cassilda nodded.

"You could not have known, Petruccio," Cassilda said. "None of us could."

Alan knelt by the dwarf.

"I am sure, Petruccio, that the oneiric pigment exists. I swear to you, I will help you find it."

At this, a grin split Petruccio's features. He clapped a hand on Alan's shoulder.

"Then I shall follow you to the ends of the universe if need be, Alan Chambers!"

Alan smiled and nodded.

He stood and walked towards Cassilda. She had healed remarkably quickly—even her teeth had returned—it could only be the powerful magic within her. Alan suspected this meant that Cali likewise was already recovering from her wounds.

She smiled coyly at Alan as he sat down beside her.

"Well, you are a singer of songs now, as well."

"It was your voice that lifted us."

"But I would not have been able to sing without you," she said. "You . . . inspired me."

Alan grinned.

"Now *that* is something I have never heard before."

"You should hear it more often. There is much about you that is inspirational."

Uncomfortable, Alan changed topics.

"Your song . . . it's haunting, and sad, but when we sang it together, I heard another side of it, a kind of strange hope, rising to the stars . . . "

Cassilda smiled.

"I wrote it a long time ago. And it has been sung many times by many singers since. But you are perhaps the first to see there is hope in it, however dim. I suppose that is the secret of Carcosa. Hope lives there, even if it is in a form that is displeasing to the eye."

Alan smiled.

"What now?"

"We must go back to Carcosa," Cassilda sighed. "Warn my Father . . . "

"Cali is well-loved by the people," Petruccio said. "By the time we arrive, no one will believe us. She will have warned the city of our coming. We cannot return there."

Cassilda looked deeply wounded by those words, but she nodded her head, accepting their truth.

"Where, then?"

"The city of Alar," LeBarron said, still with his eyes closed.

Cassilda hissed at the name.

"You are mad."

"Yes," LeBarron said. "But it is the last place they would expect. They cannot reach us there."

Petruccio considered.

"I have not searched Alar for the oneiric pigment. It's said they have a great library . . . "

"See," LeBarron said. "It really is the best course for us all."

Alan sensed LeBarron might have other reasons for suggesting the city—reasons he was not at present letting on—but he decided that he had to trust all of these souls, for only together had they prevailed.

"Well then, we set off for Alar," Alan said. "But didn't Cali say the city is underwater?"

"It is," LeBarron said. "Which is a point in its favour, as far as staying out of the way is concerned."

Their journey back was harsher than their outgoing journey in some respects, for they no longer had the aid of the quinels to carry their equipment. The marshes were just as fecund and hostile, and yet Alan sensed that the creatures of Yhtill no longer wished to contend with them. Perhaps it was The Claw. He sensed power within himself, and it was perhaps no stretch of imagination to suppose that the wildlife around them could also sense that power. He wondered if a Geiger counter would crackle if they held it near him.

At night, Alan found it hard to sleep. The sharp talons of his new appendage meant he could not easily sleep on his side or front. He had to lie on his back, staring up at the night sky. Still, the constellations soothed him. He found their configuration more pleasing than those of Earth. *Truly, you are home,* the voice would whisper in his ear, just before dreaming took him.

One night, he awoke and saw LeBarron rising from his bed. Feeling a sense of disturbing deja vu, Alan followed him off into the night. LeBarron walked for some time, eventually finding a cope of hollowgrass. He bent over and violently heaved blood into the bush. A guttering moan escaped his lips. Then he vomited again, more blood splattering the flora.

"LeBarron," Alan said.

The actor wheeled, staring at him with blood-flecked lips and cocaine-white eyes. He looked delirious.

"You follow me?" he hissed.

"I was worried. Your wound . . . "

"Will heal," the actor said. Already he was straightening, putting on the performance of wellness. But Alan had seen the truth.

"LeBarron, you need urgent medical attention. Perhaps by now the curse will have worn off and Cassilda's magic can aid you."

LeBarron shook his head.

"It was a Pe'karian blade, Alan. Coated in Pe'karian bile. Nothing in Pe'kar wears off. No demons are exorcised there. Nothing ever ends—at least, not suffering. I have been there, once. I did not tell you all before, because . . . " LeBarron frowned. "Because I suppose it felt powerful to hold back some aspect of myself. I performed there, before the throne of the Lord. Only once . . . " He shuddered, so violently Alan thought he might throw up again, but he managed to steady himself. "You cannot imagine what an awful place it is, Alan. What an awful being Pe'kar is. Disgustingly beautiful . . . " Alan could not make sense of those words. "That Cali would ally herself with them . . . " LeBarron trailed off. Alan put a steadying hand—his left—on LeBarron's shoulder.

"You are a great man, LeBarron. Full of wonders. You tricked a greater demon into relinquishing its prize."

LeBarron laughed.

"I don't think Namtar was deceived for a single second. He played along with the ritual because he knew it was the only way he could escape his confinement without breaking his vows. Demons are more cunning than we can ever conceive. I will be very surprised if he has flown to new lands, telling of the return of Haercus from the dead."

Alan stared down at the glittering talisman now latched to his arm. Perhaps that was the voice he could hear? If it was Haercus, he chose to remain silent at this moment.

"Will you . . . be okay?" Alan said.

LeBarron shrugged.

THE CLAW OF CRAVING

"I don't know. It could be weeks, months, even years. Perhaps if Pe'kar is killed his poison will wear off. Perhaps not. This is a land of mysteries, Alan." LeBarron grinned, feverishly. "And now you are one of them."

The actor walked past Alan back towards the camp, where their fire had guttered to a waspish yellow glow. Alan stood there a while longer, pondering all LeBarron had said.

The next morning, they walked until they saw the black disc of Lake Hali. Alan did not know why, but tears fell from his eyes upon seeing it—relief and uncertainty mixed like bad alchemy in his guts.

LeBarron revealed more of their plan.

"We must circle to where those large yellow flowers bloom."

"Xanthimums," Petruccio said.

"Yes. They are our entrance to Alar."

They camped that night by Lake Hali, a stone's throw from where they had camped the first night they departed Carcosa—when things had been very different. Alan awoke abruptly again and found Cassilda stood silently over him. Her smile invited him in a way words never could.

He followed her to the same copse of trees by the Lake where he had voyeuristically watched LeBarron and Cali's liaison. His heart pounded in his chest in rhythm with the Lake's quixotic tides.

Cassilda turned to face him. Her dress was crimson and black, no longer a bridal gown, perhaps a funeral one? Mourning the loss of a sister, the loss of innocence. But her pale face shone with the same moony radiance, her eyes glittering and deep, her hair like spun flax. Though her wounds had healed, her features were not quite the same. Their delicacy remained, but it had become a more pronounced elegance, as though she had been clay in need of deeper sculpture.

Their breath misted before them.

"Why have you brought me here?" he whispered.

"Is it not obvious?"

Alan swallowed.

"Obvious things elude me," he admitted. "And I struggle to know my dreams from reality, my fantasies from what's truly there . . . "

Cassilda smiled.

"Then you have come to the right place. For here, fantasy is real, and what you think of as real . . . is merely illusion."

She made him feel extraordinary things, things not of the body but the spirit. Yet, the spirit needed to be expressed, and its medium of expression was the body . . .

"I want to thank you," she said. "You . . . You have shown me new ways. You are brave, gentle, and kind." Her hands stroked his chest. God, her touch was impossibly soft.

"I want *you* . . . " she said. There was no formal dialect. The word *you* on her lips, uttered with such intensity gave him shivers. He realised she had taken off her mask for him—and wondered at how astoundingly brave that was.

It seemed to be happening in a dream, and like a dream the intensity of every aspect of the encounter was heightened: the moonlight refracting on Lake Hali's black surface, the sound of its waters lapping the shore, the brilliant brightness of Cassilda's face. When their lips touched, he went to some other place, beyond the world, beyond Carcosa, beyond the stars. He felt all his life he had languished separated from some cosmic source and only now did he rejoin it, to the blare of silver trumpets welcoming him home. Here he was. Here and now arrived. Here and now finally and eternally one. His darkness enfolded her light and swept it up as a storm sweeps bright leaves from a tree, but the leaves are not lost, they become part of the storm, revealing the darkness to be secret gold.

When they parted, Cassilda and he were both breathless.

"Now *that* is a kiss," she said. "One I have waited eons for."

"How long is an eon?" he said, his idiotic mind still whirring in the midst of this beauty. Perhaps, he reasoned, he would simply keel over and die if his brain didn't keep up its inanities.

Cassilda grinned.

"A *very* long time."

They kissed again, and Alan felt his soul melting, like snow beneath the first light of spring. As it ran, pure liquid, it joined the cosmic tributary, and that tributary was Cassilda. He tasted her power, her beauty, the secret softness of her. His left hand, un-maimed, rose and gripped her shoulder, pulling her closer to him. She bit his lips with a fury that enflamed his every atom.

At last they parted again. They remained there, holding one another for long moments. Aldebaran winked above them, a silent witness. A kiss under a Black Star.

"Cassilda?" he said.

"Yes?"

"I've found what I was looking for," he whispered.

EPILOGUE

CALI ARRIVED WEARY and wounded back at the palace of Carcosa. Unlike her sister, her injuries had not healed quickly. There were scars upon her skin, livid and yellow, lightning-forked, that glowed under a full moon. Sometimes they burned, seemingly without cause, as though merely to torment her with reminders of failure. The Claw had marked her deeply.

Curse Alan, curse him! But truly she wished to curse herself for ever showing him the way to Carcosa. She had been a fool, blinded by her ambition, not seeing what was happening right under her nose. She had given him too much, led him too far down the path, shown him more than he ever needed to see. He had awakened his true inner Self. And she, idiot that she was, had been his catalyst. She would not make the same mistake again.

However, things were looking up. She had reached the city long before them, and now she would be able to turn it against her sister and her "friends". With all of Carcosa by her side, it would be easy to dispose of them. And then, of course, to open its doors to Pe'kar when he inevitably invaded.

As she approached the palace doors, she was greeted by a flustered Eric. He looked even more the fool than usual, his hat not quite on straight, sweat dappling his chubby cheeks.

"Your majesty, your majesty, you have returned at the perfect time!"

Cali rolled her eyes.

"What new bureaucracy will you bring before me, Eric?"

The courtier did not look remotely wounded by her words, which gave her the impression his news, perhaps, was truly urgent.

"No, Princess Cali, *He* is awake!"

Her blood froze in her veins.

"What?"

"Yes!" Eric trilled, terrified. "He is asking after His daughters. Quickly, here He comes!"

And then, without warning, He was in their midst. Or rather, their midst became *Him,* such was the magnitude of His presence and power, it overwhelmed all else. The universe fell away and left only His sigil, indomitable and all-encompassing. Godhead. Divinity. These words so often on the tongues of men and women but so rarely understood. His absoluteness was a wound, a desecration of reality. He was a cut, a rend, yet also that which sealed the wound, that which filled it up forever and ever. He was the universe hermaphroditically making love with itself: disgusting, fascinating, arousing, sacred all at once.

Cali—despite all her powers and schemes and rebellious heart—fell to her knees in abrogation as the lord of all Carcosa came forth from the vast, brooding abyss . . .

The King In Yellow had returned.

THE STORY WILL CONTINUE IN
BOOK TWO:
THE CITY OF CORPSES . . .

THE CITY OF CORPSES

The Second Book Of Lost Carcosa

PROLOGUE

T HE SCOUT TRAVELLED a hundred leagues from the dismal swamps of Yhtill, over the dreaming deserts of Demhe, and at last into the land of Blue Light, the abode of Pe'kar, the Six Ringed City, the Magnificence of Ages, the Enclave of Eternity, the Court of the Demon King.

The scout was a master of his craft, having trained long eons in the service of his master, and even the likes of Cali and Cassilda had not been able to detect his presence. He had observed the party ever since they dispatched the warband of Pe'karian soldiers. He had seen them enter the Temple of Namtar, and then leave, bearing The Claw.

"Cali has failed you, my Lord." The scout knelt in the great courtroom of Pe'kar. A thousand, thousand eyes fixed upon him, their scrutiny more agonising than nine-tail lashes. But nothing in their judging eyes could compare to that of the Demon King himself.

The scout could not look directly at the Lord, for to do so would be to abandon sanity, to cast his mind into the empyrean with no hope of ever returning. The Six Ringed City's streets were littered with the gibbering, mad souls who had dared to look upon their

Lord. Only the strongest of demonkind could comprehend his majesty, his beauty, his magnificence, and remain anchored in the realm of soil and sand. The scout was not hubristic enough to believe he was one of the strongest. So he served Pe'kar with eyes downcast. The only thing he could see was a turquoise light that emitted from the throne, stabbing the pupils with its intensity.

"And The Claw," the scout added. "It has been recovered by an outcast from Earth."

Pe'kar's Shadow stretched across the stone tiles of the courtroom as a murmur went about the hall. The Shadow did not obey the dimensions and proportions of its master, nor did its movements align with his. The scout had heard Pe'kar often conversed with his Shadow. Apparently, it was the only being of sufficient intelligence to stimulate the god in true conversation. Or so the legend went.

The turquoise light changed to green, a green so horribly saturated that the scout felt like he might void his stomach over the royal flagstones. He fought with all his will to keep his food down.

"This is . . . unfortunate . . . "

The scout choked. The voice—it was so resonant, so sweet, so *perfect*. Though like all Pe'karians, the scout had long ago been gelded. He felt a tingling sensation where his genitals had once been, a memory of desire so powerful it could almost make him whole. The urge to look at his master overwhelmed him.

"Thank you for your service, honoured scout."

The scout prostrated himself, touching his forehead to the stone, as much to restrain himself from gazing upon his Lord as a gesture of obeisance. The scout remained with his face planted on the stone flagstones for what felt like hours, each second ticking by with the slowness of a nightmare. He sobbed with the effort of resistance. The voice and light, they were siren-songs, the whispers and moans of a lover, parental praise, all of these at once.

"You want to look," the Lord said.

"I cannot, my Lord. I am not strong enough. Your beauty . . . "

"But you have served well. You deserve a reward."

"Please, my Lord . . . I wish to continue to serve you . . . "

"And you shall. Look upon me."

Slowly, with the agonising pleasure of relinquished restraint, the scout began to lift his eyes. Blue, green, and white lights seeped into his pupils, stinging through the corneas, entering into the brain, and once there, blasting neural pathways, washing the jelly of his mind with poisons sweeter than honey. As he lifted his heavy lids the final microcosmic distance, to behold his Lord fully, the scout inhaled a sharp breath—orgasmic, fleeting, beautiful yet transient as a butterfly landing upon a broad leaf—and instantly his heart stopped. He keeled over and lay dead upon the courtroom floor. His face remained contorted in an expression of pure ecstasy.

Pe'kar rose from his throne, and slowly the entire courtroom filled with sickening, multicoloured light. The courtiers cheered and applauded, content to wash in his glory, forgetting their own excrescences in the cold illumination of his fell loveliness.

"Raise Haercus from the dungeons," the Lord commanded. *"I have in mind a task for him. And rally the second legion. Carcosa is weak. This time, it shall fall."*

"Long live Pe'kar!" the voices called, their multitude shaking the foundations of the black planet. "Long live Pe'kar! Long live Pe'kar!"

CHAPTER 1:

THE RETURN OF THE KING

CALI KNELT BEFORE the King In Yellow. The overwhelming potency of His aura pressed upon her like the gravity of a fell star. His approach threatened to expose all the defences she had put in place to conceal her intentions and emotions. *Bury the truth,* she thought, *bury it deep, let no trace of it remain, cast it out! You are the loving daughter! You are the loving daughter . . .*

But then even her thoughts washed away, like a sandcastle consumed by the onrushing tide. The King's psychic presence was an ocean, vast, tumultuous, merciless, and deeper than any vault. She wondered how Eric, the foppish courtier dressed in motley, could bear standing so close to the King as he was.

Unlike Pe'Kar, who allowed his naked splendour to enchant all, the King wore a tattered robe, concealing a cyclopean form that no one—save for Camilla—had ever gazed upon. Layers upon layers of grey, reeking folds entombed shadows and secrets. Perhaps he resembled a man, perhaps something altogether stranger. He stood ten feet tall, conveying a sense of colossal enormity but also rake-thin anorexia. His movements were painfully slow—it was easy to understand why. He had lived through eons upon eons, known the world when it was a seed. Or so the stories went.

Lies, Cali thought, *He made himself into a god. But even He has an end . . .* The strength of the thought almost caused her mask to slip, but she caught herself just in time, once again practicing the telesmatic ritual of forgetting—a practice she learned in her studies in the deep West, in the lands of Blue Light. One took a thought, an intention, an idea, transformed it into sigillography, then cast the sigil into the void, later to be retrieved, its power increased tenfold. It was the only method she knew of that could conceal her inner mind from the King. The void was her only escape from Carcosa's Lord.

"Dear daughter," the King said.

Cali lifted her eyes. The affection in His voice unnerved her. Ever she had been the black sheep of the family, in form and function. Ever He had shown favour towards her sister, Cassilda. But here, He honoured her with a term of endearment. Cynicism and desire for approval warred within her.

"Father," she whispered. Her breathless awe would have irritated her, had she the presence of mind for self-consciousness, but before Him, thinking became difficult. Cali had stood before many powerful beings in her time. She had killed a few of them. But none, not even Pe'kar, had an aura like that of the Yellow King.

"Thou art troubled." A statement, no question on his lips. If, indeed, there were lips beneath the cowl of that tenebrous, filthy hood. One thing she had never understood about her father was why He chose to dress like a hermit—less than a hermit, like a coprophage of the lowest order clad in shit-stained robes. Perhaps it was some gesture of humility? She did not think Him capable of that. There had to be some other reason. He was secrecy personified, a lord of mysteries, His every word concealing ten beneath, His every deed a smokescreen for some other act performed with the hidden hand. "And wounded," he continued, concern weighing his voice with granitic sincerity. "What has happened, Cali? I have slept too long."

"Do not blame yourself, my Lord," Eric stammered.

The King waved a hand and Eric fell silent, lowering his eyes. Foolish, but not stupid.

Cali's mind raced. It seemed He had not detected her deception. Yet, she could not be certain. His affection towards her was unusual, suspicious. But then again, perhaps such a display was designed to draw her out of hiding, make her crack . . . She had spent her life navigating the labyrinth of her father's crooked emotional designs. Always He seemed one step ahead. She begrudgingly had to admit her own ability to create plans came from Him.

And it did you no good, she thought. *Your plans failed.*

"What failed?" The King demanded, responding directly to her thoughts.

Cali swallowed down her alarm that she had come so close to revealing her true nature. She teetered upon the edge of a precipice. One false move and she would plunge into an oblivion deeper and blacker than anything imaginable. She could still fulfill her mission, if she held course.

"Father . . . I struggle to even begin . . . " The image of Cassilda rose within her mind, pale and slight like a moonbeam, a storm surrounding her. The angry, accusatory words she spoke rang in Cali's ears. *O sister, thou hast overplayed thy hand.* The rage frothed and boiled. She felt her wounds—the lightning-shaped scars criss-crossing over her ebony flesh—aching with remembrance. She could use this pain to mask what had really happened. "Cassilda . . . she has betrayed us, betrayed *you.*"

A terrifying silence followed her pronouncement. Though she could see no eyes—a strange reality of her life, that she had never once looked her father *in the eye*—she could feel His immense scrutiny, punishing as an avalanche.

"Betrayed?" He repeated, quietly. "My beautiful Cassilda, the image of her mother . . . *betrayed?*"

The titanic stones of the palace trembled. Cali would not have been surprised to learn that everywhere across Carcosa the church-bells had begun ringing their dirge in sympathy for his betrayal.

The King turned away from Cali. Moving across the stone tiles with concealed limbs. Eric could not conceal his horror at the news. He had always been Cassilda's pet.

"My favourite daughter . . . " the King whispered. "A traitor in blood?"

Cali trembled like the palace, the rage a toxin in her veins. She hated Him, but this anger was directed inward for being stupid enough, *weak* enough, to think He had changed for a moment. She could not control the circumstances of her birth. And in fact it had been *His* fault, His sin, that had brought her into being.

Cali was the offspring of her father's infidelity, her mother being a succubus who had seduced the King many eons ago. She was therefore a child of two worlds. Strangely, she thought of Alan Chambers in that moment. Perhaps that was why she had been so lenient with him, had not seen what he was becoming until it was too late. She wondered where he was now. The group would have fled. If they returned to Carcosa, Cali would make sure they were seized. But she doubted Cassilda would be stupid enough to do so.

She knew how Cali held favour with the people, if not with her father and the court. So, where would she have gone?

"Where is she?" the King asked. He had turned back to face her, not that any face was visible. Once again Cali was reminded of how careful she had to be with her thoughts.

"I do not know, father," Cali said.

"We must find her. We must bring her back. I must question her myself . . . "

Cali would do all she could to avoid that happening, for if the King probed Cassilda's mind, He would discern the truth in short order. Still, she could play along for now.

The King drew closer to Cali and extended a dishevelled sleeve. A digit—perhaps a finger, perhaps something more octopean—touched her chin through the gauze of soiled cloth. It was all she could do to conceal her revulsion and disgust. He lifted her chin so that she stared up into the impenetrable blackness of His hood. The closest they had ever come, perhaps, to emotional intimacy.

"Did she give thee thy wounds?"

Eric averted his eyes, stood awkwardly to one side, not wishing to eavesdrop, but not yet dismissed by his master.

"No," Cali answered, swallowing down bile. "It was another, one Alan Chambers, an outcast. I regret that I brought him to this world. He held great promise. I thought that . . . he could do great things." No theatre was required here. She truly felt all these things and more. They said actors drew on lived experience to make their dramas believable.

Now she found herself thinking about LeBarron, the actor who had helped them get to the Temple of Namtar. She remembered the night of passion they had shared—then his betrayal. What sane man would give up her to ally themselves with a demented pervert like Alan Chambers? Who would follow a gimp over a goddess? Yet he had chosen him, not her, at the critical moment. And it had spelled her undoing.

"He has The Claw, father," Cali finished.

"The Claw?" the King hissed. "Cali, thou hast truly overstepped thy bounds."

It wounded Cali doubly to realise how similar Cassilda and her father were, what kindred high falutin terms they thought and spoke in. The rage, suppressed as it had to be, had condensed into an ingot of solid loathing, a physical thing in the pit of her stomach.

THE CITY OF CORPSES

Forever Cassilda and the King reminded Cali of how she had overstepped, overplayed, gone too far. They placed limits on her— and on Carcosa itself. For all their magic, they were narrow-minded beings. Cali would surpass them. She would—

A deep breath quelled the thoughts and banished them into the abyss. She would suffer for this magic later, when it returned tenfold in power, but for now her true aims would remain undetected.

"I have failed you, father," she said, projecting every bit the image of the repentant daughter. "It was in my efforts to please you that I overstepped my bounds. I desired to bring you a champion, a hero of the same legend as Haercus, one who could wield the Claw and defeat Pe'kar." She took a deep breath. The outpouring of emotion had once again become very real, and she did not want too much of that truth to spill. "But I misjudged, in my fervour, in my devotion . . . " She broke down into inconsolable weeping. This, too, was real in its own way. Her wounds pained her. The bright yellow scars would likely never truly heal. The Claw marked reality, that was its power. It was the mechanism by which mortals could change the universe. Her only consolation was that Alan would, like Haercus, likely be driven mad by its power. Only by removing the Claw had Haercus escaped insanity, and not long afterward he had been captured by Pe'kar. Stories of his death were spread to the far corners of the black planet, but Cali had learned the truth in the land of Blue Light, that Haercus lived, imprisoned in the deepest of Pe'kar's dungeons, his mind—already on the brink of collapse—overthrown by the Demon King's esoteric devices of torture.

"Hush now, dear daughter," the King said. "I have treated thee harshly in the past . . . "

Cali looked up, tears scalding her with almost as much fury as her wounds. Did she hear regret in His voice? Repentance? A flood of emotions broke through the dam that the solid ingot of hate had stoppered. If He truly were to ask for her forgiveness, if He were to acknowledge His failures as a father, then perhaps she could forgive him, and perhaps there would be no need for her to overthrow Carcosa. If He was capable of change, then she would much rather see that change than risk the city she loved so well under the armies of Pe'kar. Nothing she had done could not be undone . . . yet.

The Yellow King's oppressive aura increased in intensity, until it felt as though she were in a wind-tunnel, barely able to remain upright even though kneeling and close to the ground.

"Father?" she murmured, unsure what this change portended. Was this His love for her, rising? Was this what it felt like to be loved by the King In Yellow? To be at the centre of His cyclone? To be accepted by father and god? It took all her restraint not to cry out in joy, to throw her arms open, to cast herself upon Him, embracing His filthy robe.

"I have treated thee harshly in the past . . . but now thou shalt know *agonies* for thy failure."

Cali's eyes widened with shock. A second later she was thrown back and pinned to the ground by a force so colossal it seemed the planet itself had fallen upon her. She screamed and then convulsed as invisible power coruscated over her limbs. Ten thousand volts, a hundred thousand, were not equal to this. Every atom of her being vibrated at an infernal frequency. Her mind felt like it had liquefied. Her limbs threatened to fly from their sockets. The seizure was so great that white foam erupted past her lips. Her screams gargled under the bodily fluid. Her brain felt as though it was being squeezed by two tectonic plates. She was a grub in His disgusting fingers. A beetle beneath His heel. Nothing.

He had punished her like this before, of course, but always there had been an end point. She had grown accustomed to knowing when He would relent. Now, there was no cessation. Even her screams died as the pain became transcendental. Her eyes rolled into the back of her head as her limbs thudded against the stone floor. No man had ever pressed himself physically upon her without her consent, but this was a higher form of rape, her soul squeezed in a death grip. What manner of being was her father that He could asphyxiate the stuff of spirit?

Blindness took her. Then loss of hearing. Thus, she did not see or hear Eric weeping as he watched her twitching form. Nor did she see her father's eyes, blazing out of the darkness of His cowl like two yellow stars in the gutter of outer space, the omens of their malicious shine unreadable to even the wisest of seers.

Join Blood Bound Books
Newsletter for updates on book
two and to receive 20% off your
next order at
www.Blood BoundBooks.com

ACKNOWLEDGEMENTS

This book also could not exist without the inspiration provided by Brian Barr. Brian Barr's *King In Yellow: Stories Set In The Robert W. Chambers Mythos* is simply an incredible collection of tales, and an awe-inspiringly original take on the mythos. He brought Carcosa back to life in my mind, he paved the way, and had I not read his stories, I don't think I would have had the courage to take on this epic tale.

Without the palaeontological advice of Edward Kennard, the marshes of Yhtill would not have been half so interesting to explore. He genuinely blew my mind with some of the obscure creatures he conjured from the depths of prehistory. Ed is an amazing writer and a dear friend. My life is so much brighter now that he's in it.

There is more sex in this book than any book I've ever written, and this is probably only just the beginning. For this, three people are to blame: Clive Barker, the great master of the fantastically sexual; Christa Wojciechowski, whose incredible erotic scenes gave me the courage to try writing them myself—a journey of self discovery; and S. C. Mendes and Nikki Noir, who showed me that the horrifying and erotic often intersect.

And finally, always, thanks to my wife, the secret flower of Carcosa, in whom the dew of inspiration is sweetest and most profound.

ABOUT THE AUTHOR

Joseph Sale writes dark fantasy and epic poetry. He has authored more than ten novels. He grew up in the Lovecraftian seaside town of Bournemouth.

His short fiction has appeared in *Tales from the Shadow Booth,* edited by Dan Coxon, as well as in *Idle Ink, Silver Blade, Fiction Vortex, Nonbinary Review, Edgar Allan Poet* and *Storgy Magazine.* His stories have also appeared in anthologies such as *Blood Bank* (Blood Bound Books), *Lost Voices* (The Writing Collective), *Technological Horror* (Dark Hall Press), *Burnt Fur* (Blood Bound Books) and *Exit Earth* (Storgy) alongside writers such as Richard Thomas and Neil Gaiman. In 2017 he was nominated for The Guardian's 'Not The Booker' prize.

You can chat with him on Twitter @josephwordsmith, or, if you want to go deeper down the rabbit hole, you can sign up to his newsletter for a free eBook novella: http://themindflayer.com

Made in the USA
Las Vegas, NV
16 February 2025

18213471R00090